Trusting
Love Again

Starla Kaye

ISBN 978-1-936556-71-7

Trusting Love Again Copyright 2015 Starla Kaye
Cover design Copyright 2015 R. J. Savage

Published 2015
Printed by Black Velvet Seductions Publishing
A division of Savage Publications

Visit us at:
www.blackvelvetseductions.com

Chapter One

A tear trickled down Toni's cheek, then another one. She dashed at them with shaking hands. She'd lost so much, and now this. It was too much to bear, especially on this bitterly cold mid-February day. This situation was all wrong.

Another glance from where she sat in the long driveway of the two-story Victorian house broke her heart. Every inch of the large house, turret, gazebo, and porch had been painted stark white. From her childhood days here in Petersville, Kansas, she'd dreamt of the fading turquoise house with the fancy trim in varying shades of pastel colors. It had always seemed magical to her.

During the miserable ride from Denver back to her roots two days ago, on Valentine's Day - worst day of the year ever, in her opinion - she'd forced aside her losses and concentrated on her future; *this* house. She'd endured awful months from June through December while waiting for her divorce to be finalized. What had kept her sane and kept her moving forward was this house. It had been vacant for as long as she could remember. She'd believed that it had needed her to be reborn as much as she did.

Her dream had been violated, like she had.

In October, Donald Caruthers, the realtor she'd found who represented the Carter family who owned the property, had told her that there were still some complicated legal issues to get settled. He hadn't gone into them really. He'd just said that he was pushing hard for the people involved to get everything settled between them so a clear title could be signed. He'd assured her that she would get it, as long as she could be patient a little while longer. Then he'd suggested that, if she would make a substantial down payment, the people holding things up would take that as a good sign, and that everything would move along faster. She'd been suspicious, but he'd always sounded so positive every time she talked to him on the phone. Finally, she'd given in and done as he'd advised. Stupidly.

She gritted her teeth and tried to calm down. She was tired of being a victim.

Two weeks ago, Caruthers had said there were only some minor legal matters with one of the relatives left to deal with. He'd told her that she could move into the detached carriage house that had a remodeled apartment above it. Again, she'd been concerned. Yet when she'd received the key a couple of days ago, she'd packed up what little she had at the condo in Denver, checked on her furniture in storage, and headed here.

Minor legal matters? She blinked tears of frustration. He hadn't said a word about anyone else being involved in the sale. Certainly nothing about someone having made changes to the main structure, or about someone having moved into the house.

Not a house now, a business. One with a sign planted in the flowerbed in front of the long, covered porch: *Anderson and Anderson, Attorneys at Law.*

She'd been lied to yet again.

Only twenty-seven, her belief in love had been shattered already. And now this supposedly kind-hearted older man she'd not actually talked to face-to-face had cheated her. She'd been right to be suspicious. Her trust in men was seriously damaged.

Yes, she should have checked Caruthers out more. She'd never handled any kind of business on her own, but she thought she could manage this. And he'd seemed so helpful.

She climbed out of the hot red Mustang she'd purchased with money from her hard-fought-for divorce settlement and carefully closed the door. Darn it all; she'd been violated, mistreated for the last damned time.

Aching clear to her soul, she marched up the sidewalk, intending to have words with the man she felt certain was responsible for the abomination: Chad Anderson. She hadn't thought about her brother's long-time friend in years. Although he was five years older than her, they had a complicated history. Mostly, he'd seen her as an annoyance, except he'd seemed to like when they'd disagreed about things. Early hints of his becoming a lawyer like his father. She'd had a ridiculous attraction to the good-looking, older boy. Now she didn't care what he looked like. Now she simply wanted him not to be messing with her new life.

The lackluster square white sign with its black lettering caught her attention. *No, no, no!*

She set her purse on the ground. Sucking in a breath of irritation, she turned sideways, lifted her arms up by her chest, balanced on her right leg, and then did a roundhouse kick with the ball of her foot right into the center of the words, yelling, "Hai ya!"

The wooden sign broke in half, each part crashing back against the porch railing with a loud thump! Her former karate instructor would be so proud. Unfortunately, the stiletto heel of her shoe had broken off, taking some of the pleasure out of the moment. She'd really liked these Christian Louboutin patent leather pumps, even if the five-inch heels made her wobble a bit at times.

Balancing awkwardly on the damaged shoe, she bent to pick up the heel and her purse. At the same instant, the front door opened and two people rushed outside. A stunned-looking twenty-something pregnant woman gaped at her first. The man she'd intended to have words with shifted by her until he could glower down at Toni from the steps.

"What the hell have you done?" Chad growled, his face tight with fury. He strode down the steps, an iPad or tablet or whatever held firmly in one hand. "You haven't been back in town two days and already you're making trouble."

Her breath hitched at the anger in his deep baritone voice; an automatic response. Her heart pounded. Her stomach knotted and she hobbled backward. It took a second for her to regain control and remember this wasn't Stanley. Her ex-husband wasn't getting ready to attack her again. She shoved those horrible memories aside and concentrated on where she was and who had spoken.

Chad knew she was in Petersville again? Of course he did. Her brother must have told him.

She stiffened and walked right up to him, tears of anger and weariness stinging her eyes. The gangly but handsome teenage boy she'd had a crush on was gone. He'd always been a lot taller than her, but now he was well-toned and definitely all mature man. He filled out a dress shirt in an impressive manner. Awareness and physical interest tingled inside her in a way it hadn't in a long time, surprising and unsettling her.

Appalled with her body's response to him, she motioned to the Victorian as fury surged through her. "You've mutilated *my* house."

A thick, dark eyebrow lifted. "Mutilated?" His forehead knitted in vexation. "*Your* house? What are you talking about?"

The young woman inched closer, worry creasing her face. Even as Toni noted that, Chad's gray-haired, still striking father and law partner walked onto the porch as well. She heard an engine as another car drove up and stopped behind her. A door opened and closed. She didn't bother to look back at whoever had arrived.

"Antoinette," Chad prodded, talking in a clipped tone.

He knew she hated that name, as much as he didn't like being called Chadwin. Her redheaded temper, held under rigid control during the six years of her disastrous marriage, broke free. "*Chadwin* Anderson, you knew how much this house meant to me. I used to talk about it all of the time."

"You were a child. Kids have silly ideas," he said in dismissal.

Even if that might be true of some kids, this had been an important dream of hers. It had stayed with her ever since she'd foolishly run away to get married in Las Vegas on her twenty-first birthday. Somehow, it had been her link-pin to her hometown and to the family she'd disappointed and barely spoken to since. Many times she'd talked about returning here to somehow make peace with her family, but Stanley had always talked her out of it. He'd controlled her in so many ways. Plus she'd been raised to believe that you fought for your marriage. She'd done her best for as long as she could; longer than she should have.

God, she'd been so weak-willed, so naïve in her trust of the wrong person.

But this wasn't the time to think about him or her other reasons for coming home.

"You've taken my one surviving dream and ruined it. You…" The rest of her rant got clogged up in her throat.

His expression softened and he watched her with wariness. "Ted mentioned that you've had a bad time recently, but…"

"*A bad time?*" She'd been emotionally battered and bruised by her lying, cheating ex-husband. After their break-up, their marital problems had been dragged through the Denver society pages. She'd been made out to be the one completely at fault.

"You can't possibly know all that I've been through! Nobody here knows." She didn't want to think about how far past 'bad' things had gotten. But she was glad that her shame wouldn't have spread to her hometown. At least she hoped it hadn't.

He glanced at the young woman standing close by, worrying her lower lip. "Maybe you should call…"

"What? Call my father? Because I'm acting a little wild?" Toni snorted and cut him off. "I have every right to act upset. Yet *another* man has messed with me; lied to me."

His angular face tightened in annoyance. "I still have no idea what you're talking about." He stepped closer and reached for her.

"No!" She jumped back, breaking off the other stiletto heel, and barely managed to keep from falling. Her entire body tensed.

A memory flashed into her mind. Stanley had grabbed her arms during their last argument, right after they'd eaten a special meal she'd prepared for him. His grip had been agonizingly tight. When she'd hissed in pain, he'd shoved her away. She'd landed hard on the floor, knocking her head against the dining room table. After a half-second of possible regret, he'd turned and hurried out of the house. No apology.

"Antoinette," Chad said again, sounding cautious.

She pushed the recollection away and looked at Chad. His expression appeared concerned. Again, he inched forward and tried to reach for her.

"Don't touch me!" she gasped, batting his hand away, dropping the heel and purse. She hated that she was reacting this way but felt helpless to control it.

"What's your problem?" Appearing confused, he moved toward her once more.

Panicked, defensive, and determined to stop him, she snagged the iPad from his grasp, flung it away. It crashed into the nearby towering, leafless elm tree. The sound of cracking glass made her flinch. *What had she done?*

Footsteps behind her on the sidewalk pounded in her direction. The young woman on the porch gasped and Chad's father walked behind him.

"Have you been drinking?" Chad's tone dripped with disgust as he seemed to sniff for hints of alcohol.

Her cheeks flamed. "No, I haven't been!" she bit out. It was humiliating to realize that her brother must have told Chad about her drinking problem; something he must have read in the gossip columns.

His vivid blue eyes didn't look as though he believed her. His jaw taut, he latched onto her left forearm before she could move. He gripped her tightly.

No! Panicked, she drew on the self-defense lessons she'd learned after the separation. With a palm strike, she gave a hard jab to his shoulder.

"What the hell?" he snapped, jerking but not releasing her. His arm was stretched out between them.

Heart racing, she hit his elbow with another palm strike. This time he lost his grasp on her arm and glowered at her in frustration and pain. She sensed he would reach for her again, but she couldn't let it happen.

She balanced on her left leg, raised her right leg to shoulder level, the denim of her jeans tight with the position. She raised her arms in a protective position and kicked at his chest with all her power.

He crashed backward against the broken wooden sign, lost his footing, and landed against the side of the porch. Despite the horrified gasps of the young woman and Chad's father, Toni heard the sound of a bone cracking when he hit one of the sign posts. She gaped in horror at the sight of blood oozing down his cheek from where his face hit the porch edge.

"Oh my God," she whispered shakily, rushing toward him.

Sitting amidst the broken wood and dirt of the garden, he straightened as best he could manage. His face tight with agony, he roared, "Stay away from me!"

She jumped back, arms windmilling to keep from falling on her broken shoes. Her heart pounded harder, shocked at the damage she'd caused.

His father and the young woman hurried to his side to help him up. Both looked at her in warning. Her legs felt weak and she fought to keep standing. She didn't even recognize the woman she'd become. Never in her life had she hurt someone else.

The steady footsteps stopped their approach and someone grabbed at her left arm. Again, instinctively, she spun around, her hands shooting out in defense. "No!"

A man she recognized as another of her brother's friends sat on his butt at her feet, dazed, rubbing at his jaw. "Toni, calm down," he ordered.

The fight drained out of her like a balloon suddenly jabbed with a pin. She began trembling. Tears of shame threatened as she watched Alex Crampton; *Sheriff* Crampton climb to his feet. The broad-shouldered, mountain of a man watched her with molten brown eyes, as if weighing whether she would attack him again. It sickened her that he would be thinking that way. Yet she couldn't blame him.

"That's better." He seemed to consider the situation for an instant, and then he pulled handcuffs from a clip on his belt. "You're under arrest, Mrs. Beaton," he said formally.

He didn't look happy about it, resigned, and he clamped the cold metal cuffs over her wrists. She was too numb to resist.

"Ms. Thornton," she corrected automatically. As confused as she was, she never wanted to be connected to that name again.

Could her day - her life - get any worse? "I,I didn't mean to…" She hung her head in disgrace. There was no denying what she'd done; there were so many witnesses, including the sheriff, who she'd grown up with. Swallowing hard, she asked in a whisper, "Are you taking me to jail?"

He looked hesitant and then they all heard Chad grousing in pain, "She's a menace."

That hurt. She needed to help him somehow, make him understand. But understand what? Even she couldn't comprehend her actions. She'd known Chad all of her life, except for the years of her marriage. He'd never been a fighter; never hurt anyone that she knew about. Yet she'd turned on him in a moment of distress. She'd used the defensive skills she'd learned to cause damage to property…and to injure an innocent man. Away from that panicked moment, she knew he hadn't meant her harm.

"Your family isn't going to like this," the sheriff said on a heavy sigh. He didn't like it, either.

Reality hit hard. She could barely breathe, she felt cold all over. She was going to jail. Her family would be seriously unhappy with her. Not any more than she was with herself, though.

She offered a heartfelt but shaky, "I'm sorry." After what she'd done, she didn't consider the apology enough. And from Chad's hard expression, he didn't either.

Unable to stay there an instant longer, she glanced at the sheriff, determined to think of him in that capacity, not as someone she'd known forever. "Let's go. Now."

***

"This can end here," Alex said, as he opened the back door of the patrol car, looking down at her uneasily. "I'm sure Chad…"

Toni shook her head, tipped out her chin. "He was right. I deserve to be locked up." Although the idea made her almost sick.

She felt sorry for herself during the short ride downtown to the sheriff's office. Chad Anderson had cheated her; his father, too. They were involved in some kind of evil plot with the realtor to destroy her happiness. Chad thought she was a drunk, a menace to society.

But when the car stopped in front of the sheriff's office, the excuses for her behavior faded away. *She* had done wrong and there was no one else to blame.

Alex helped her carefully out of the car. He'd been bigger than most of his peers all of his life; could look intimidating just because of his size, but he was a gentle soul. It seemed odd that someone like him would become an officer of the law. Yet she also sensed a harder side to him that hadn't been there the last time she'd seen him. She knew he'd gone into the marines at the same time her brother and Chad had gone off to college. For a second, she wondered what had happened to change him, what internal baggage he carried around. Everyone had some; she certainly did.

As they stepped away from the patrol car, a middle-aged couple walked by on the sidewalk toward the Dine-In Café a couple of buildings down the street. Toni's face flamed as she recognized the members of her father's church. No doubt news would spread quickly among his congregation that Reverend Thomas Thornton's mischief-making daughter was back in town and in trouble again. *Perfect.*

"Come on," Alex said, lowering his rumbly tone. "Let's get you inside before anyone else wanders by."

Bearing up to her shame, she hurried toward the office door. From the corner of her eye, she noted how the couple had stopped to stare. She still had the handcuffs on, although Alex had wanted to remove them before she'd climbed into the backseat of the car. He'd been annoyed that she wouldn't allow it. Now she wished she hadn't been so stubborn.

She stopped in the middle of the open area with a pair of worn desks belonging to the deputy who worked the next shift and to the sixty-something receptionist.

Bella Hampton pursed her lips and shot Alex an are-you-serious glower. "Really? You arrested her?" She gave Toni a sympathetic look.

Toni sensed his discomfort as he moved behind her to unlock the handcuffs. "I didn't have a lot of choice," he muttered. "Call her father to come take her home."

Bella reached for the phone, but Toni faced him and protested, "Did I damage someone's property? Did I injure someone? Did I…" She couldn't believe she was insisting that she actually be tossed into the jail cell. But, darn it, she had done wrong and hated herself for it. She needed a time out, adult style.

"Toni, I'm sure you can work this out with Chad and his father," Alex countered, his tone strained. "They're reasonable men."

"Well, Chadwin didn't appear all that reasonable when he called me a *menace*," she grumbled, still wounded by the comment. She desperately wanted to sit down and do a bit of pouting.

"Chadwin?" Alex questioned, amusement ringing in his voice. One corner of his mouth lifted. "I believe you're the only one who ever got away with calling him that."

"Not the point, Alexander." It pleased her to see him wince. He, too, disliked his real name. Tired of the distraction, she strode to the pair of empty cells and stopped in front of the first one. She didn't face either Alex or Bella, just waited.

"Dammit, Toni. You're intent on making my life hell, aren't you?" He marched next to her, then noted the red lines around her wrists from the handcuffs. "Hell! Look at what you made me do."

"I'm sure it isn't the first time you've done this to a prisoner." Why was she taunting him? She could see how much the minor injury upset him. But she was in a mood, so he could live with it.

"Never to a woman. Never to the sister of one of my best friends." He looked miserable, but he opened the door and let her walk past him. "Call her father. Call her brother. Call anybody."

She went to sit on the narrow bench and started shaking. Yet she met his eyes and said obstinately, "Don't you have paperwork to fill out? Fingerprints to take?"

He ground his jaw and took a second before he said, "If I fill out paperwork, then this is going to get real serious, real fast. You'll have to go in front of a judge. You'll need a lawyer." He looked at her as if he wondered if she really were crazy. "No fingerprints."

Her stomach roiled. "If you didn't know me, what would you be doing now?"

"Dangit, Toni!" he grumbled and then closed the cell door. He barked over his shoulder to Bella, "Call her father!" He focused on her once more. "What lawyer do you want to call?"

Oh, what had she gotten herself into? Why hadn't she just let him release her? "I, I don't know who to call," she stated meekly.

***

When his doorbell rang at home several hours later, Chad wasn't in the best of moods. Even with the pain medication, his broken left forearm hurt like hell. The side of his cheek stung from the half dozen stitches, too. He didn't want to talk to anyone at the moment.

Disgruntled from his injuries and from a wasted day of work, he pulled the door open to find one of his closest friends standing uneasily on the porch. It wasn't Ted's fault about any of this, but still he frowned as he motioned him inside.

Ted glanced at the cast and the temporary sling, then at the bandage on Chad's face. "Damn. I'm so sorry." His shoulders slumped inside his heavy coat. "We knew Toni is a troubled woman now, but... Hell, man, we're all sorry."

Chad closed the door with a sigh. "She's way past *troubled*. That sister of yours has some serious mental issues. She's dangerous. She's ..."

"She probably does have some psychological issues," Ted interrupted quietly, sounding worried.

His friend's admission surprised him. He'd only made the comment because he was frustrated, in pain, and had been stunned at her odd behavior. "I don't really think she's dangerous. I just..." He stopped talking, uncertain exactly what he thought at the moment.

Ted straightened to his full height, looking Chad square in the eye. "She isn't dangerous, not really. Evidently that was a 'last straw' moment for her."

"I gathered that." She'd had a temper in the past, but never anything like that. What he couldn't forget was the way her eyes had widened in genuine fear when he'd touched her.

"She's hardly told us anything about her marriage; about what went wrong," Ted said, pulling Chad from his musings. Ted's expression showed true concern. His hands fisted at his sides. "We think the sonofabitch abused her."

It took a second for that to register in Chad's mind. "Beaton beat her?"

He couldn't imagine the vibrant, fiercely independent woman allowing anyone to do such a horrific thing to her. Not the young woman who used to tease and torment him every chance she got, or argue with him about anything and everything. She stood up for herself, which was part of why he'd liked her so much.

But then he was an elder abuse lawyer. He'd seen and heard of things most people could never imagine. They were inflicted on people by others who supposedly had their best interests at heart, often caretakers or loved ones. It also happened in far too many marriages. He hated to think that hers had been one of those marriages.

A vein pulsed in Ted's neck. "Possibly, but she hasn't said as much."

"Verbal abuse, then?" Chad knew that could be almost as cruel and difficult to deal with. "I can't see her taking that."

Ted's shoulders rose with a deep in-drawn breath, and then slumped. "None of us can. But, dammit, she broke down last night when we were all trying to find a way to make peace."

He pulled in a breath, but his voice still held pain as he said, "At one point she was sobbing so bad we could hardly understand her. It was clear, though, her scum of an ex had done some major damage to her psyche."

The whole idea was hard to take in. Chad would have to do some research of his own about the situation. He fought for the underdog on a daily basis. Still, it was hard to see Toni that way. He'd have to think on the matter later when his mind wasn't dulled from the pain medicine and he was a lot less frustrated with what had happened.

Speaking of that, he asked pointedly, "So, what was the deal with the place Dad and I are buying? She wasn't making much sense. Talking about how we'd mutilated *her* house. About the place being her dream." *That was the 'last straw'?*

As he'd tried to think about other things while getting his arm set and the stitches, he'd wondered about her reasoning. She'd always gone after whatever she wanted full throttle. If she'd really wanted the house all these years, he could easily see her trying whatever crazy plan came to her mind to get it. Although destruction of property - like their sign - and assault and battery seemed a stretch.

"We're fuzzy on that. She's pretty depressed right now, won't say much."

"I'm sure your Mom will…" Chad stopped when he caught the frown on his friend's face. "What else?"

Ted heaved a breath that seemed to come clear from his toes. "She's still in jail."

"What?"

"Still in jail."

Chad gaped at him. "Surely Crampton didn't…"

Ted nodded. "Yes, he did." Disgust filled his face.

"Alex actually arrested her? Wasn't hauling her away in cuffs enough?" He couldn't believe Alex would have done such a thing. They were all friends, even Toni. Even a bit crazy Toni.

"My idiot sister insisted on it. She pressed him to do it no matter what he tried to tell her." Ted looked more frustrated with his stubborn younger sister than Chad ever remembered seeing him. "The last I heard she was waiting for an attorney, except she doesn't know who to call."

Well, hell. Chad knew exactly who to call. He strode into the living room and straight to the end table where he'd set down his cell phone. Grumbling under his breath, he held the phone awkwardly in his good hand and thumbed in his Dad's number.

He didn't have a chance to speak before his father said, "Already on it, son, but it hasn't been easy. Little Ms. Toni thought it was a conflict of interest for me to represent her. It took some doing, but her father finally convinced her to let me do so."

"I'm going to have some words with Crampton tomorrow," Chad said, feeling a headache that wasn't related to his injuries coming on. He would call the judge, too, to get this matter dropped. "Thanks, Dad."

When he disconnected and glanced at Ted, he found his friend grinning in amusement. "What's so funny?"

"She still gets to you, doesn't she?"

Chad remembered the night after his divorce and how he and Ted had gone out drinking. It wasn't something he normally did, but he'd been a broken man that night. His ex-wife had shown a bitter, selfish side he'd never witnessed until that day. Pleased with being free again and with getting a hell of a settlement, she'd stopped him in the hallway outside the courtroom and admitted that she'd had an abortion several months before. She had a career in fashion design she planned to pursue and didn't want to be burdened with a child to care for. She'd told him that since he was such a workaholic that he'd make a terrible father. So she'd made both of their lives easier.

Drunker than he'd ever been before, he'd told his friend about it. In his stupor, he'd told Ted that he'd never really loved Sandy. That he'd been in lust over Toni for years, until she'd run off to marry Stanley Beaton. Between her betrayal and Sandy's betrayal, he'd sworn that he'd never trust another woman with his heart. Ted had denied that his sister had betrayed him, since they'd never actually dated. Logic hadn't mattered then. He'd moved on from that point. Sandy had been right:

his life revolved solely around his work.

"Those feelings are long gone." Even if the first sight of her in six years had about stolen his breath. He cared only about her welfare now because she was his friend's sister. Nothing more. *Right. Who was he kidding?*

Ted gave him a disbelieving look and moved toward the door. "She's going to need help, that's all I'm saying. Cut her some slack, okay?"

Chad took a second before saying, "I'll try." *God, what a mess.*

Chapter Two

From her childhood bed, Toni stared at the ceiling in her old bedroom and found comfort in the dark. What an awful day it had been! She'd had such hopes for starting a new life and burying her rocky past where she never had to face it again. All she'd wanted was to come home to Petersville, throw herself into remodeling the beloved Victorian house, and find her internal happy place once more. She wanted to adopt a cat or two; felines as independent and spirited as she'd been before Stanley. He'd done his best to destroy who she'd been at heart. Darn the lousiest excuse for a man!

God, what she'd done today wasn't a good sign. It made her feel sick just thinking about everything. She was afraid it would take longer than she'd like to become "normal" again; sane.

If only her parents had told her that Chad and his father had moved their business into the house, she wouldn't be in this mess. No, that wasn't fair.

None of them had known she'd obsessed about this fantasy for most of her life. Sure, she'd talked about the abandoned house reverently, because it reminded her of a magical place. She'd always loved the fancy trim with the Victorian scrolls. As a child, many times she'd snuck over to the house and onto the wide, covered porch that wrapped the front and most of one side. The gazebo on one corner had fascinated her, as had the rounded three-story high turret. Back then, the house had badly needed painting and repairs. No one seemed to care about the house, except her. She'd even overheard some people in town calling it an eyesore that should be torn down.

First thing tomorrow she would call that lying, cheating realtor. She'd paid a lot of money already with the assurance that everything would be cleaned up with the title before long. It appeared that the Andersons had been somehow lied to and cheated, too, although they were attorneys. You'd have thought they were smarter than that. Evidently, the realtor was a real sneaky bastard, not the compassionate and helpful man he'd presented to her. She wondered if the actual owners even knew what was going on.

"Are you all right, sweetheart?" Her mother gave a quiet knock on the closed door and then opened it to peek inside the room. "We've been worried about you. You didn't even eat supper before you came up here."

Toni jerked upright, clamping a hand to her hammering heart from the surprise visit. "Yes, I'm fine," she said in a rush. She wasn't, though. "I needed some time to myself."

She hadn't wanted to replay with her family the horrific details of what she'd done and about going to jail. They already knew, anyway, other than knowing *why* she'd snapped. She was too embarrassed to talk about it. If only the whole incident could just be forgotten... But it couldn't. She still had repercussions from the incident to deal with.

The savory, spicy scents of the Italian meal she had been unable to eat earlier still lingered in the house. In the light from the hallway, she saw concern creasing her mother's softly lined face. "We just want you to know that we love you."

Toni swallowed hard at the distress in her mother's voice. "Thanks, Mom."

Her mother probably expected to be invited into the room so they could discuss the matter. In the past they'd had many conversations here about so many things. They'd been close, even though she had tended to get into a lot of mischief with her friends during her teen years. And then she'd disappointed her parents; gone against them. She'd been so sure that Stanley Beaton, of the powerful Denver family, was the best man who would ever want her. Now, because of her bad decisions, she and her family were uncomfortable with each other. She regretted that. But she wasn't up to talking right now.

"I'm really tired," she said and lay back, hoping to be left alone peacefully. She wanted to get close to her mother again; just not yet.

"Okay, dear," her mother's tone held sadness and hope. "We can talk tomorrow."

"Sure, Mom. Tomorrow."

As the door closed again, Toni heaved a sigh. She wished she hadn't broken down last night and revealed anything about her disastrous marriage. But she'd been tired from the stress of the last eight months, from driving all day, and from facing her family again. She didn't remember exactly what had pushed her over the emotional edge, or what she'd said as she'd sobbed uncontrollably until she'd managed to run upstairs to be alone. Something about Stanley's terrible temper, about him calling her vile names. What she did remember were her mother and brother's horrified expressions. And the devastation on her father's face; as if he should have protected her somehow and failed.

She knew that her family wanted to know more about what she'd gone through in her marriage. They wanted to be there for her now; take care of her. That's what families did for each other. But she was ashamed of all of it; more ashamed of not having listened to their counsel when she should have. This was her problem alone to get beyond.

The situation from today was, as well. The violence in her marriage was not an excuse for the vicious behavior she'd shown today. She had to woman up and take control of her life; be responsible for her actions.

She'd been so irresponsible in the past, so blinded by Stanley's attention…by what he offered her. He'd promised her a life that she would never have been able to experience here in small town Kansas. What had she really gotten? Ruined.

Her reputation had been shattered by lies, lies, and more lies. She'd suffered through six months of pure hell while struggling to divorce a man who had wronged her. She'd faced more than skepticism about her accusations. No one had believed her at first. It hadn't been easy finding an attorney who would even take her on as a client and file for a divorce. The Beatons were that influential.

Divorce. Just thinking of it was still difficult. Not the reality of it, but doing it…giving up on her marriage. You were supposed to love, honor, and obey. You were supposed to do that for the rest of your life. Or so she had been raised to believe. In spite of all that she'd gone through with Stanley, going against her beliefs had been hard.

Benjamin Hoolihan, the gray-haired, elderly lawyer she'd finally hired had, surprisingly, played hardball with Stanley and his family. He hadn't been in awe of them as so many of the upper echelon in the city had been. He'd managed to get her more of a settlement than she'd even considered. She had enough money to last her a lifetime, if she was wise with her investments. All she'd wanted was to be free of the man who hadn't really loved her, hadn't honored their marriage vows, and obeyed no one but himself.

She curled her hands into fists, the nails digging into her palms. His betrayal of their marriage vows had shredded her pride. She had endured a lot during their last few unhappy years together. She'd left here a foolish, rebellious, starry-eyed young woman with no set purpose in her life other than getting away from here. She returned disillusioned, heart-bruised, and broken in spirit.

That wouldn't last.

Drawing in a steadying breath, she went over the goals she and her therapist had worked out together: get her emotions leveled, find a new focus, and possibly get a job. Most importantly she would rebuild her self-confidence. Okay, she had a lot of work ahead of her, but she would get there.

***

The next morning, Toni braved another bone-chilling day to make her way to the Municipal Clerk's Office. Snow had started to fall when she'd pulled into the parking lot. She would like to simply stay here in her warm car instead of facing the humiliating next hour or so. That wasn't an option.

She turned off the engine, forced a calmness that was shaky at best, and stepped out of the Mustang. A blast of cold air hit her and she pulled her coat tighter around her. Why hadn't she longed to visit Hawaii or some other nice warm place instead of wanting to come back to her hometown? Not only was the weather pitiful at the moment, but also she had so many unpleasant memories to face here.

Enough! It was time to face the consequences of her disgraceful actions the day before. She was a grown woman who needed to act like one.

As she entered the older, slightly musky smelling County Courthouse, she experienced a moment of relief with being back into somewhere warm. She unbuttoned her calf-length wool coat and studied the building's directory nearby until she found the location of the clerk's office. On leaden feet, she made her way to the second floor.

Her stomach tightening, hands feeling clammy, she pulled the big glass door open. But she couldn't move further toward the chest-high wooden counter that spanned most of the back wall. Only one woman stood behind it: Mrs. Agatha Trousdale. Toni had known the sixty-something widow all of her life. Mrs. Trousdale knew pretty much every act of mischief she'd been part of. Even now the older woman frowned in disapproval.

"Bring it here, Antoinette," Mrs. Trousdale commanded, motioning Toni forward.

Toni tightly gripped the citation she had received yesterday afternoon. She drew in an anxious breath and walked grimly across the small room. Her heels clattered on the tiled floor. Without meeting the clerk's eyes, she slid the document across the worn counter. She'd hoped that no one besides the clerk would be here, although she suspected at least half the town already knew about her being arrested, handcuffed, and taken to the sheriff's office. That was life in a small town.

As she scanned the citation, Mrs. Trousdale tsk-tsked. She did some complicated stamping thing and turned to the copier behind her. "I imagine your father had quite a lot to say about this latest bit of trouble."

In truth he hadn't said much. She felt even worse because he hadn't lectured her. She didn't respond, instead accepted the copy the woman handed to her.

"No doubt your poor mother received many phone calls about your latest misbehavior." The older woman shook her head of short white hair and pinned Toni with a chastising look. "She's had years of experience with that."

Pushed to the limits of her patience and respect for elders, Toni glowered back. Then she asked abruptly, "I go to the courtroom now, right?"

She felt slightly nauseous and her knees grew weak. What a mess. Why hadn't she been able to control her temper? Her therapist would probably say she was still in the recovery stage after the abusive relationship; still unable to deal with acting and reacting on her own, without being told what to do after so long a time. An excuse, but not one even she could accept. She deserved this.

Mrs. Trousdale nodded. "You shouldn't have long to wait for your sentencing. There was only one other offender being arraigned this morning." Her gaze finally softened. "I assume your father's attorney explained what happens next?"

"Yes."

The act of simply getting an attorney had been a bad experience, although less so than it had been in Denver. She hadn't known who in town to contact. Her father had wanted her to use his good friend, Ethan Anderson. That had seemed wrong, since she'd attacked Ethan's son. In the end, Ethan had convinced her to let him represent her. Oddly, he'd been a bit amused by the situation. He'd mentioned about his son needing something to upset his rigid world, needing a challenge to face besides his work. She still didn't understand his reasoning. Beyond that curious comment, he'd carefully gone over the arraignment today; how she would face the judge on her own, and what her probable sentence would be.

She turned on her heel and left the small office. Almost smothered in the coat, she removed it and draped it over her arm. Again she had to force her feet to move down the hallway toward her goal. She went over what she'd been told by Ethan. There would be a fine to pay, as well as the expense for Chad's new iPad, and his medical bills. At least she probably wouldn't have to serve a jail sentence. She might have to do community service, which was all right. She would do anything to put this all behind her.

When this was settled, she needed to move on with her new life. She didn't relish the idea of living at her parents' home any longer than necessary, though she appreciated them taking her in after their last, unhappy parting. She desired a place of her own. For the time being, that place was supposed to have been the carriage house's apartment behind the Victorian house. Yet another problem she had to figure out.

She also wanted to find a job, but that would have to wait until after whatever sentence she received. Getting a job wouldn't be easy. She'd worked in fast-food places the summers of her high school years. College hadn't really interested her, other than a minor interest in marketing, so it had been easy for her to quit after eloping with Stanley. He'd insisted on her being a stay-at-home wife. At the beginning, that was okay. Basically she had no workable skills.

She sighed. There would be more "poor me" time later.

To her unpleasant surprise, the instant she opened the wide wooden doors to the courtroom she spotted her antagonist, the reason she was here today: Chadwin Anderson. Okay, that wasn't true. He hadn't actually done anything wrong, other than moving his firm into the house she'd planned to buy. At some point she needed to find out how that had come about. But it kind of helped at the moment to see him as partly at fault for her ridiculous behavior.

This had to be *the* most embarrassing moment of her life.

Well, next to being arrested and handcuffed in front of his law office on one of the town's busiest streets. She now had a criminal record - even if this was only a minor offense. She would have this mortifying black mark against her previously unblemished reputation forever. Unless she went through the process of Expungement to have the record sealed. What was the point here where nearly everyone in town would already know about it?

She took a seat at the back of the courtroom in the gallery, setting her coat and purse on the bench beside her as quietly as possible. Disturbing the judge talking with the day's first offender wouldn't be good. She tried to avoid glancing at Chad, but it was impossible. At least he wasn't looking in her direction as she studied him awkwardly. He had a cast on his left forearm. A bandage covered part of the left side of his face, over the stitches the cut had required. Her stomach churned. They might be at odds, but she regretted having injured him.

Her thoughts went to what Ethan had said about her possible pleas. *Not guilty* meant she would have to face another court date; have witnesses involved. Witnesses that she knew would not be on her side in this situation. *No contest* didn't seem to fit either. She couldn't have legal counsel and, if found guilty, the judge could impose a maximum sentence, which probably would be worse than what she might face if she pled *guilty*. This was really a lose-lose situation…and entirely her fault.

Before she had time to calm her nerves, the first offender grumbled as he strode out of the courtroom.

"The defendant, Antoinette Grace Thornton, will now approach the bench."

She blinked, unable to stand, feeling faint.

The middle-aged, balding judge looked at her and frowned.

Still she couldn't make her body cooperate.

"You don't want to annoy the judge," Chad said flatly from across the aisle.

Irritated at his intervention, she stood and walked with brisk steps to the left side of the bench.

Chad watched the color return to Toni's face and breathed in relief. When he'd seen how pale and frightened she'd looked as she'd entered the courtroom, he'd had the crazy urge to go to her. He wanted to take her in his embrace and promise her that everything would be fine. He hated this whole situation. Still, she'd brought this all on herself.

With her proud chin raised, she walked right up to the judge's bench. But her hands were fidgeting with the sides of her skirt. When she'd walked by him, he'd almost been able to smell her fear. In spite of his being the one accosted, he worried about her.

Ever since she'd run away and gotten married all those years ago, he tried not to think about her or encourage conversations about her with her brother. He'd had personal reasons for being hurt by what she'd done. His feelings for her had always colored his relationships with other women, especially with his ex-wife. In a way, he'd been comfortable with his anger with her, with his irritation that she'd been the beautiful young princess in the powerful Beaton family and not with him. But now he knew that her "perfect" marriage had been far from that.

As he watched her trying to face the judge bravely, he thought about how he'd gone on the Internet early this morning when he hadn't been able to sleep. What he'd found made him sick. It hadn't taken him long to realize how much she'd been manipulated by her ex and his family. She'd been used, socially abused. She'd been accused of marrying for money and, maybe she had. But she'd been young, probably blinded by what Beaton could offer her. When he'd found a small article that mentioned her having been physically attacked, an article that had shifted to basically calling her a liar, he'd been outraged. She might have gotten into more than her share of mischief in the past, but she'd never been a liar. His gut told him that hadn't changed. Even now, he wanted to find the asshole that had hurt her and beat the hell out of him. He wasn't normally a violent man, but this was different.

"Ms. Thornton, you are charged with multiple misdemeanors. You are charged with disorderly conduct, engaging in violent behavior that resulted in injury to Chadwin Anderson." The judge glanced in his direction and pulled him back to the present.

Toni shifted to look at him as well. She winced, worrying her lower lip as their gazes locked. He noted the regret in her expression, helplessness, before she faced the judge again.

Her behavior hadn't been *that* violent, although at the time he'd thought so. He remembered Ted telling him about how she'd reluctantly admitted to her family that Beaton had verbally abused her. Ted had suspected there had been physical abuse as well. It had repulsed him when he'd heard that. Now that he knew more from research, he felt even worse. The sonofabitch had destroyed the free-spirited, fun loving, always smiling young girl he'd once known. The girl he'd argued with time and again, actually enjoying the disagreements. The young woman he'd desired and lost because he'd been stupid about not revealing his budding feelings for her. Now it was too late. They'd both suffered in bad marriages and he wasn't willing to take another chance. He couldn't imagine that she would be either. Plus, his life was complete already; he had a job that consumed him, which he enjoyed.

The judge cleared his throat and brought Chad back to the moment, again. "You are also charged with criminal mischief, knowingly damaging property that belongs to another person. In this case, an iPad belonging to Chadwin Anderson, as well as to a sign belonging to the Anderson and Anderson law firm."

Toni's shoulders slumped. He wished he could stop this, but it was out of his hands at this point.

"Do you understand the charges, Ms. Thornton?"

"Yes," Toni whispered loud enough for him to hear.

"What is your plea, Ms. Thornton. Not guilty. No contest. Guilty?" He looked intently at her. "I assume you have been told the differences."

Toni nodded, took a second, and said, "Guilty, Your Honor."

Chad waited as anxiously as Toni, who shifted uneasily. He knew the possible sentences and had already spoken to the judge, first in an attempt to have the charges dropped. When that hadn't been accepted, he'd suggested a possible sentence that he could live with.

"You will pay a fine of $150 on each of the three charges, for a total of $450." The judge gave Toni a stern look. "I know your history in this town as a teenager, and I know your family."

Chad fought to stay seated, wanting to defend Toni somehow. Many in the town had disapproved of the almost constant mischief she'd gotten into in her teenage years. Nothing had ever been harmful to anyone or anything. The worst incident being when they'd filled the baptistery with powdered strawberry drink. She just got carried away sometimes and ran around with a group of mischief-makers. He didn't think she should be judged by her past.

Toni trembled, making him worry about her fainting or something.

"I could sentence you to thirty days in jail." The judge hesitated and slowly looked understanding. "Several people have come to me on your behalf."

Who? He had, of course. *But who were the others?* Possibly his father. Maybe her brother; a town councilman. Maybe her father. Whoever they were, he was grateful.

Toni remained silent.

"Ms. Thornton, I sentence you to thirty days of community service; 240 hours." He glanced at Chad. "Is this acceptable to you, Mr. Anderson?"

He stood. Toni turned to look at him, clearly wondering. "Yes, Your Honor."

"You are also in agreement with having Ms. Thornton perform her community service by working for your law firm?"

Toni's eyes widened and she tensed.

"Yes, your Honor."

"Ms. Thornton, you will begin your sentence tomorrow." With that, the judge pounded his gavel on the bench and got up to leave.

Instead of being happy with the light, easy sentence, Toni shot Chad a sizzling look. It would be an interesting thirty days.

Chapter Three

After spending the rest of the day driving almost mindlessly around Petersville, the countryside, even to the nearest town and back, Toni was exhausted. She'd had to absorb the awful humiliation in the courtroom. Even more so the sentence she'd received. She hadn't been ready to face her family, who had not been in the courtroom that morning, at her request. But they would have heard the outcome. She didn't doubt that many people in town who lived on the gossip grapevine had heard by now as well. A thought that made her remember the couple on the street who had witnessed her being taken to jail.

She took her seat at the dining room table, determined to eat with her family and deal with them at last. Putting the cloth napkin carefully over her lap, she raised her gaze to look at her mother sitting across from her. Her mother's eyes held so much sadness that she fought the need to escape to the safety of her bedroom. She'd caused her this worry, this pain.

She couldn't look at her father. How many times could a good, decent man bear being disappointed by his daughter? She'd been an often headstrong brat as a teen, and he'd dealt with the issues over and over with amazing patience. Then she'd been at her most rebellious stage when she'd opposed them about Stanley. And she'd never once contacted her family while her marriage had grown worse and worse, not even when it had blown up. Even though her parents had a good marriage and believed in making it work, her father would have tried everything he could to help her. She'd known that, but she had been too devastated and embarrassed to approach him. Now she'd been unable to control her temper, damaged property and injured someone. She honestly didn't know how to make it right with him, or with any of her family.

The uneasy silence frayed her nerves. She couldn't eat, even though her mother had made all of her favorites. Her plate was full of roast beef cooked to perfection, not too well done and not too juicy. Green beans in a creamy sauce sat beside the mashed sweet potatoes she used to love. She'd yet to take even one bite. No one else at the table seemed to be eating, either.

Suddenly her mother broke the quiet. "Have I mentioned how happy I am that you're home?" Her eyes held such worry.

Her mother had said it in many ways, at least a dozen times since Toni walked in their front door three days ago. She nodded, glancing at her still vivacious mother. At fifty-five, her mother could pass for a woman in her forties. But tonight, with regret weighing heavily on her, Mary Thornton looked older than her years. Toni hated that, certain she was at fault.

"I'm sorry, Mom." She stopped not knowing exactly what she should have done, what she *could* have done differently.

She'd made her disheveled marital bed and been forced to accept it. Marriage to Stanley had been a marriage to both him and his influential family. The experience had changed her. They'd molded her to fit their needs and she'd been in such reverence of them that she'd accepted it all. He'd needed her to be hostess extraordinaire at times, simple eye candy accompanying him at others. Somehow, she'd ended up on social committees for groups she hadn't even believed in or liked. It had always been about Stanley and his family. She'd seen it as being about making her marriage work.

She caught a look of loving and concern move between her parents. She'd wanted their kind of relationship. Instead of respect from her husband, she'd gotten disgust at her naivety to his lifestyle, then verbal abuse. Instead of tender touches, he'd given her an occasional "playful" pinch on her bottom that had hurt. Or a quick peck on the cheek before he left the house for work, if he even bothered with that. Instead of allowing her to show her temper, or dare to argue with him, he'd get furious. He'd even slapped her a few times when he thought she'd gone against him. Then he'd tried to soothe the physical and emotional wound away by giving her a hard and unwanted kiss. But there'd never, ever been the simple love so easily displayed by her parents.

Studying her plate, but not really seeing it, she regretted not calling her parents back when her marriage started turning bad. Especially her Mom. She'd needed to talk to her, but couldn't. Shame and wounded pride were awful things sometimes.

"I should have…" Again, she stopped. All the "should haves" didn't matter.

"Yes, you should have…-" her father started gruffly.

"Thomas, no," her mother countered. "Let her tell us when she's ready."

"Mom's right, Dad," Ted added. "We shouldn't push Toni to talk to us." But he looked like he really wanted her to open up to them.

Would she ever be ready to talk to them about her marriage? About what had happened? She hadn't actually talked about any of it with anyone other than her attorney and the therapist he had found for her. But she really hadn't had anyone in Denver to discuss anything with. No friends of her own. And in their circle of friends as a couple, she'd been made out to be the one who'd destroyed their "perfect" marriage. According to *his* friends, his family, and the reporters who had savored every lying detail he'd supplied them, there hadn't been even a hint at the abusive man he could be at times. For that she'd been glad. It would have been even more humiliating.

She forced those unpleasant memories away and looked from her determined mother to her worried father and to her concerned brother. "I hate that I'm making all of you suffer because of me. These are my issues to deal with, not yours. I shouldn't have come here. I…"

Her father frowned, his eyes filled with grief. "Of course you should have! We're your family."

Her mother nodded, as did Ted.

"I don't deserve any of you." Before anyone could respond, she went on, "But I'm glad you're here for me. And I'll be okay. I promise." She pulled in an uncomfortable breath and blew it out again. "After I get this community service matter behind me."

Her parents exchanged a look. She hadn't yet told them about the sentence, but they knew, just as she'd suspected they would.

"It was a fair decree," her father said. "Community service, even 240 hours of it, isn't uncalled-for."

She carefully aligned her spoon and fork. "No, I agree."

"Having to serve those hours by working for Chad bothers you, though, doesn't it?" her mother asked quietly.

She couldn't deny it. How ironic was it that she was required to work for the man she'd injured in the place she was in the process of buying?

"Chad is a good man," her brother said from his seat next to her.

"He talked to the judge on your behalf; tried to get the charges dropped. Since the sheriff had witnessed it all, that was impossible. But give him credit, he did try."

It had been her rotten luck that Sheriff Crampton had pulled up in front of the law office at the worst of times. He'd arrived early for an appointment with Ethan, or so he'd explained on their drive to his office. He'd been hesitant at first to approach her because of his friendship with her brother and with Chad. But her initial act of resistance when he'd pulled her away from Chad hadn't helped. The struggle had been instinctive. Still, Alex hadn't wanted to actually arrest her, but in the end he'd had to. She'd forced him to do it. She would never forget hearing the sound of the handcuffs closing around her wrists; the feel of the cold metal. Worse, she feared it would be a long time before her need to panic when a man touched her like that would fade away.

She wasn't totally convinced about Chad's goodness at the moment, although he'd looked sympathetic in the courtroom. He'd also done crazy things to her, attracted her as much as he had in the past. That unsettled her. "Hopefully I'll work mainly for his father."

Her family had told her that Chad was an elder abuse attorney. Ted had explained that his friend traveled a lot; either for a case in another town, to work in his second office in Topeka, or for a speaking engagement on the subject. She'd been surprised to learn about his specialization in that field, when the last she'd known he planned to go into estate law practice like his father. She wondered what had changed his mind, although she had no intention of ever asking him.

"Ethan's proud of his son," her father said, drawing her attention. Pride in their children had always been something he and Ethan, his long-time friend, had often talked about. She knew how proud he was of Ted's success with his hardware business, and with being on the Petersville city council. His only concern with his son was that he hadn't found a good woman and settled down yet. She, too, wondered why he hadn't.

She, on the other hand, had never done anything to make her father proud of her.

Since listening to her sobbing breakdown that first night here, learning a small piece of what she'd gone through during her marriage, her parents acted warily around her. She didn't like it. She wanted things to go back to normal. But it would take a while. Especially after her misdemeanor actions, which would also affect her father. He was prominent in the community, not only as the long-standing pastor of the First Baptist Church, but also as the great-great-great-grandson of the town's founding father. Yet all he'd said at the jail when he'd come to see her was how much he loved her.

"I will deal with this, Dad." She straightened the napkin in her lap far more than necessary. "It pains me that I embarrassed you...and myself."

There was an awkward moment of silence and she couldn't look at any of them.

Then her father protested, "We're not embarrassed, sweetheart." When she glanced up, he met her gaze, his eyes troubled. "Surprised... and worried."

Ted cleared his throat. "Impressed, too. About the sign thing, not about Chad's injuries." He gave a weak smile. "Although, after hearing Alex describe your wicked karate self-defense moves, I'm impressed with that as well."

She rolled her eyes. "Seriously?" But she felt better about his attempt to lighten the situation. There had been times in the past when she and her brother had difficulties getting along, like any other siblings. But she knew in her heart that he would always be there for her. He would have been there for her if she'd even hinted at marital problems. Again, she wondered why he'd never married. What was wrong with the women in this town? He was "hot" and made a good living. Back in high school he'd never lacked for a girlfriend. In college, she'd thought he was even getting serious about someone - Sarah? Suzanne? Maybe one of these days she'd ask him about it.

***

Are you sure about this, son? About having Toni working here for the next month?"

Chad stopped pacing his office and faced his father. As usual, he couldn't interpret his facial expression. There was a hint of curiosity; of acceptance, and a bit of concern. For him...or for Antoinette Thornton? He was worried about her, too.

His arm hurt and he'd had a lot of trouble getting dressed with only one good arm. It was time for another pain pill, but he didn't want to take one. She'd done this to him in a spurt of temper. As long as he'd known her, she tended to act first and think later. But the "actions" had always been verbal; a flash of a few words to express her view on whatever annoyed her at the moment. Occasionally, those few words had become a lot more, particularly when the two of them were going nose-to-nose over something. He'd actually enjoyed their challenges; missed them after she'd left town. No other woman even thought about taking him on like that. But this "action" had been different.

"She's had a rough time," he said quietly. Where he'd believed her heartless and selfish when she'd went against her parents to marry an older man they disapproved of, he wondered about her *real* reason for doing so. He still didn't think it was all about the money. "She was too young back then. Naïve about the real world, and why people did things. I think she was blindsided by out of control hormones; lust for a man that swept her off her feet with sweet words, promises, or whatever."

Until his talk with Ted, he hadn't considered any of that. Even after reading up on their marriage via the ever helpful Internet, he still didn't understand what the socially prominent Stanley Beaton had really wanted of Toni. Even so young, she'd been a rare beauty. Spirited. Probably passionate in bed as much as she was in everything else she did. That was something he didn't want to contemplate, particularly not in connection with another man.

"I think you're right, but she's not the same person now," his father said, with sadness in his voice.

"No, she isn't." Chad ground his jaw, which tightened the stitches on his cheek and made him wince. She had matured into an even more beautiful woman; a fact that had hit him hard. He'd been attracted to her before, now... okay, even more so.

His father settled a hip on the edge of Chad's large mahogany desk and studied him. "Thomas doesn't know what to do to help her heal. And Mary...well, she's devastated about what little she's learned about her daughter's marriage."

Chad drew in a breath. Even with the occasional family tiffs over the years, mainly due to Toni's tendency to push her limits with them, they'd been close. Ted spent a lot of time being annoyed with her for one reason or another. But he defended her without hesitation to anyone speaking bad about her. He had, too, although he doubted she knew that.

"Ted told me what she admitted to them while crying, but he believes there is a hell of a lot more she hasn't shared. Probably won't." He struggled with his anger. "I did some research. They have a right to be worried about her. She had a raw deal for a long time."

Their gazes met and his father nodded, no doubt also having done some checking up about her. He was pretty sure that his father hadn't shared what he'd discovered with his old friend. Her family was hurting enough already in their concern for her.

"Some people in town are already talking about her and what she did here, and to you. They're judging her based on her foolish behavior in the past. It's going to be hard for her in town for a while."

"I know." Chad clenched his right fist in frustration. "I hate that."

His father stood; again met his gaze. "We're going to help get her through this, aren't we?"

Chad nodded. "Even if she doesn't want our help." He had to smile, thinking about the contrary young woman she'd been. "She'll resist *my* help for sure. At least I hope she will, since that will be a sign of the woman we knew returning."

***

Toni tossed and turned in bed; unable to fall asleep, troubled by what she'd done to Chad and by having to face community service working for him. There had been a time when she'd had a crush on her brother's best friend. He'd been every young girl in Petersville's dream back then. Star quarterback on the football team, he'd helped get to State his senior year in high school. Cheerleaders vied for his attention, as did every popular girl in school. But he'd only dated one girl all through school and on into his college years; Serena Hayes. Everyone had thought they would get married. They'd broken up just before his college graduation and no one knew exactly why, not even her brother.

Toni'd wanted him to notice her, but she'd been five years younger. He'd tolerated her presence at times but nothing more. From time to time, they'd disagreed on things and had heated arguments, which she'd enjoyed. But that was as far as her relationship went with him. So she'd looked for someone else who would see her as more than the pastor's mischief-making daughter, as her older brother's pest of a sister. Someone who liked her spirit - even encouraged it. Someone who found her *hot* and would let her explore her passionate nature.

Stanley Beaton had attended a party at her sorority house and somehow they'd ended up together in his apartment that night. He'd taken her virginity and, to her delight, begun dating her. He'd filled her with all kinds of foolish young girl's dreams; traveling to exotic places, going to parties with Denver's elite, wearing designer clothing and jewelry he'd buy her, and so much more. At first, his parents had objected to their dating, but he had a mind of his own. He'd wanted her and they had finally accepted her. But her parents had never accepted him.

She rolled to her stomach and hugged her pillow. Why hadn't she seen the imperfections in Stanley that her parents had? It would have saved her a lot of heartache and humiliation.

Her parents had forbidden her to date him. So, of course, she'd done just the opposite. She'd dated him without their knowledge. He'd liked that idea, telling her that he enjoyed the "wickedness of doing the forbidden." And that had appealed to her as well.

Until the night she'd come home and told her parents that they were going to elope on her twenty-first birthday. It had seemed so romantic to her. They'd argued horribly, but she'd still packed up the rest of her belongings that she'd wanted to take. She'd driven to Denver the next day and she'd thought she'd lost her family forever.

She rolled back over and decided not to think about the past any longer. Her therapist had told her to move forward with her life; to concentrate on taking one day at a time. But these next thirty days were going to be difficult. It would be awkward working for Chad, seeing him every day. Even more so if she couldn't get control of her attraction for him. *Wrong man, wrong time.* Their lives had gone in different ways and she was okay with that. Besides, he probably had a woman he was seeing now, although her brother hadn't mentioned it. She hadn't actually asked him either, and she wouldn't.

None of that mattered, because she was never ever getting involved with another man. *Remember those cats you wanted to live with.* Maybe dogs would be better. They were always so loving, so loyal.

Irrelevant. She needed to get through this community service and then focus on establishing her life here again. But, darn it, she really wanted that Victorian! *Note to self: Contact Caruthers and have a few strong words with him. Find out what the hell is going on.*

***

She moaned and writhed on the bed. He had her pinned down. Her arms were stretched out above her head, her wrists tied to the bedposts. He'd done it before, one of their more wicked games. But this time she tried to resist him. He didn't listen, believing she was playing a different role, laughing about it. But it never took long for her to relent and give in to the heat in his gaze. Even sometimes rougher than she'd like, she enjoyed being taken by her man.

She tensed, waited for what would come next.

His slim hands kneaded her breasts, hard enough to be uncomfortable, and then he pinched her nipples. Laughing as she whimpered in pain. Pinching again.

"Please don't…" But she lay there and let him do as he pleased, like always.

He tightened his fingers on one of the hard buds and then shifted down her body, until his head was at her trembling core. Continuing to grip that tortured nipple, he lowered his head. She held her breath as he ran his abrasive tongue over her pulsing clit.

Again she moaned; again she writhed. She knew what would come next, didn't want it…and yet.

He bit the swollen nub. Not hard, but firmly enough to make her cry out.

"Stop it!" he ordered, lifting his head to glower at her. "You know you like this, slut."

She looked at him as tears misted her eyes. It was a half-truth. Some days she didn't mind his forceful play. Other times she missed the gentle lover who had first made her into a real woman. He hadn't hurt her back then, hadn't gotten excited when she struggled against his more enthusiastic efforts at sex. This wasn't making love. This was raw sex, done with the intent more to please him than her.

She needed more time, sweet arousing. "Please…"

He ignored her plea. "I'm going to give you more pleasure than you can imagine," he snarled.

He didn't understand. It was too late to reason with him. She drew in a breath, tensed. He was her husband. She loved him.

Grinning smugly down at her, he shoved her knees up by her shoulders and pushed her legs further apart, until she was completely open to him. His determined gaze met hers as he moved forward, hesitated for just a second, and then drove deep inside her.

She screamed, tears sliding down her cheeks. Heaven and hell at the same time.

Toni was panting, trembling when she flashed her eyes open and stared into the darkened bedroom. Her heart raced at the vivid memory.

Shocked, worried that she'd cried out and someone might have heard her, she got up to run into her bathroom. Numbly, she washed her face off with cold water and then slumped onto the cold tile floor. What had brought this on? It certainly wasn't missing Stanley. God, no.

Dashing away her tears, she remembered how concerned Chad had looked in the courtroom. Concerned and so handsome. He was all grown up man now, decadently appealing with his thick, dark hair and those haunting blue eyes. The woman in her desired him. Not to take her as harshly as Stanley had at times. She wanted...

No, no, no! Absolutely not! What are you thinking?

She climbed to her feet and made her way back to bed. Being attracted to Chad was so wrong. After already making too many wrong choices in her life, she refused to make another one.

Chapter Four

She was late. Pressing the *snooze* button too many times after a restless night, a hair dryer that hadn't cooperated, misplaced keys, and enduring a five-minute conversation/lecture about tardiness from her mother had started her day off wrong. All excuses, flimsy ones at that.

The extra-wide driveway behind the house that served as the Anderson & Anderson office parking lot was full, adding to her annoyance. Where did they expect her to park? Refusing to leave her precious car on the busy street, she took one of the diagonal labeled spots, one reserved for "Ethan Anderson." She would try to smooth out the issue with him if he showed up later.

Toni hurried around the house to the front and dashed up the porch steps, flinching as she glanced over at the place where Chad had landed when she'd shoved him. Her pulse raced with nervous tension while she walked into the house. Maybe no one would notice her not being on time. Maybe they didn't know that the court had told to be here promptly at 8:00 am. She wasn't sure if she was supposed to report to Chad or his father, or did it even matter?

Stomach churning with unease, she took off her coat and added it to the oversized hall tree in the foyer. There was a faint scent of vanilla air freshener moving around her. She pulled in a steadying breath and headed into the sitting room that had been remade into the firm's reception area. A travesty that she tried not to let bother her.

The petite, very pregnant young woman she'd seen the other day glanced up from her desk. "Mr. Anderson - Chad, that is - left a couple of messages for you on your desk. To check later."

"My desk?" Even though this wasn't a real job, a tingle of excitement swept through Toni. She'd never had a desk of her own, partly because she'd never had an office job.

The woman motioned to another small room on the other side of the foyer. "You'll be using the copy room as your office during your time here."

Okay, the first desk of her own wasn't quite as thrilling as she'd thought.

Toni nodded, noting the hint of disapproval in the other woman's eyes. She started to move but the woman said, "I'm Ellen Yardley, the firm's secretary and receptionist. Do you prefer Antoinette? Or something else?"

"Definitely something else." She gave a smile, hoping to ease the strain between them. "I usually go by Toni."

Ellen accepted the information and glanced at her computer monitor. "Chad is in a board meeting upstairs in the conference room. The other men showed up earlier than he expected, but he wants you to help take notes. He said to send you in as soon as you got here."

She looked up, appearing puzzled. "Chad also wanted to make sure he scheduled a private meeting with you before you left for the day." She focused on the monitor again. "I put the meeting on both of your calendars for 5:30. We close at five o'clock, just so you know."

"That's fine," Toni said, feeling awkward about the 'private meeting' and the after-hours time. What could that be about? She really didn't want to be alone with him, especially after the unsettling thoughts she'd had about him last night.

She hurried to what had been a small downstairs bedroom and turned into a copy room/office and gaped in surprise. A slender vase with a couple of pink roses sat next to a monitor on a table that would evidently serve as her desk. *Roses? For me?* She couldn't remember the last time someone had given her flowers of any kind.

Drawn by the sweet scent, she stepped closer and picked up a small note beside the vase. *We'll make this work out.* The note was signed by both Chad and his father.

Ridiculously, she teared up. How could they be so nice to her? Yet she couldn't resist leaning over to smell the roses. A second later she straightened, put her purse down, and found a notepad and pen beside the keyboard. She scooped them up and hurried up the stairs and followed the sound of voices.

Her hand shook as she gave a quiet knock before taking hold of the doorknob. *Calm down. You can do this.* The pep talk didn't help much. She forced a smile, turned the knob, and walked into the meeting.

A dozen well-dressed businessmen in suits she knew from growing up here glanced at her. She thought she caught a couple of disapproving frowns, but Chad drew their attention. "If you'd look over page twenty-one for a few minutes, we'll discuss it shortly," he told the others.

As the men turned their focus to the papers on the table in front of them, Chad looked at her with a raised eyebrow as if implying "You're late. Really?" Still, he didn't appear upset, which made her relax a bit. He nodded at the chair beside him.

Reluctantly, she moved to it and sat down, her wary smile still in place. Thinking about the roses left for her, she relaxed a bit. They were attempting to make the best of the awkward situation, and she would too. She put the notepad and pen on the table and tried to act prepared. She could handle this.

But she had to be honest with him. "I'll try my best to take whatever notes you think necessary," she whispered, face burning. "You need to know that I've never been a very fast writer."

He studied her for a second, giving a hint of a smile that made him even more tempting. "I've changed my mind about the note taking," he said in his deep-timbered tone.

She sighed in relief and started to scoot her chair back.

"No. I want you to stay. Listen to what is discussed. Maybe you can help me go over it all later."

Drat. She would rather have been excused and allowed to get back to her little office. She needed distance from this man who confused her. Instead, she settled into her seat once more and gave a curt nod of agreement.

Before he looked away, she saw his nostrils flare, those blue, blue eyes warmed. Or was she imagining it? In the next second, he shifted his attention to the papers in front of him and appeared to forget her presence.

It wasn't that easy to dismiss him, though. She noticed that he needed a haircut. A thick lock of nearly black hair fell onto his forehead. She found it sexy. *Totally inappropriate.* That didn't keep her from wanting to touch the curl and slide her fingers through his hair. Even back in her teen years she'd been fascinated by his always slightly scruffy hair.

She blinked, her face heating, hoping nobody noticed. These were not the kind of thoughts she should be having.

He got excited, impassioned about something in the papers, and she watched him curiously. He pulled in a breath that tightened the short sleeved dress shirt he wore to compensate for the cast on his left forearm. That was when she realized the other men wore jackets while he didn't. As she looked guiltily from his arm in a cast to his face again, she grimaced at the sight of the small bandage on his left cheek. He'd suffered because of her fit of temper.

Oh God. She was a terrible person.

The other men joined in the discussion, with Chad going into minute details over some kind of re-zoning issue for a proposed parking lot the group wanted. After a few minutes, all she heard was *blah, blah, blah.*

Her mind drifted away to something of more interest to her personally. She tried to find anything in her recent past that she could put on a resume. Depressing. With her limited skills, her work future looked unpleasant. What was she going to do? She didn't need to work, but she couldn't see herself sitting idly around. She still wanted to buy this house, but that possibility was even more complicated than it had been before. She recalled her mental note about calling Caruthers. Tonight. She wanted to set up an actual face-to-face meeting with him.

"Okay, good meeting," Chad announced and jerked her back to the moment. He nudged her foot at the same time and, when he glanced sideways at her, she caught the hint of amusement in his knowing gaze.

The men closed the folders in front of them and began scooting back chairs and standing. A couple looked in her direction, then at Chad. It was obvious that everyone in the room knew why she was here and wondered why he had agreed to the sentence, since he'd been the injured party. She didn't understand his reasoning either, unless it was his effort at acknowledging a victory of sorts. But that didn't feel right.

One of the oldest men in the group, a paunchy man she recognized as a deacon from her father's church, walked toward her. His gaze was assessing, as if he were comparing her to the young woman he remembered. While she tensed for his condemnation, his eyes softened and he extended his hand, "It's good to have you back in town, Antoinette."

Surprised, she had to force herself to stand and shake his hand. Did he feel her palm sweating? Sense how nervous she was? "Thank you," she managed.

She wasn't sure what to do now, but she hoped none of the others wanted to speak to her privately as well. This was an awkward situation for many reasons. She slid her glance to Chad, seeking his help.

He picked up her notepad and pen and handed them to her, a gentle smile on his wounded, carved face. "I believe Ellen has some things she needs assistance with. We'll talk later."

"Yes, of course. Ellen."

She walked out of the room, leaving Chad and the older man behind. They talked casually about the last time they'd played golf together. She hadn't known Chad golfed, but then she didn't know anything about the man he'd become, other than about the focus of his side of the law practice. It was something that intrigued her.

Why had he decided to go into defending the elderly in abuse cases? From her own experience in an abusive relationship, she knew how difficult the situation could be. It would take a very special, understanding person to deal with people who had suffered from physical, emotional, or sexual abuse, or from being exploited or abandoned by those who were supposed to care for them.

She ended up having all day to settle into her temporary job. Ellen kept her busy with filing, making endless copies for a workshop Chad was to give next week, and with trying to figure out the time management program. Ethan hadn't come in due to outside meetings in the neighboring small town, which was a reprieve. She'd not been sure how to face him after this mess she'd made for them all. And Chad had spent the day scrambling from one client meeting to another. She'd had far too much time to worry about the private meeting with him after work ended for the day. And too much time to smell the roses, to wonder whose idea it had been to get them for her. They were the bright spot of her day. In truth, the bright spot in her life over the last eight months.

She was scowling at the monitor, frustrated with trying to retype a legal document for Ethan, when Ellen popped into her doorway. She had a hand to her lower back and discomfort creased her pretty face. The poor woman was due to give birth any day now and more than ready, as she'd told Toni several times during the day.

"I'm leaving, and I'll lock the outside door." Her hand moved to her bloated stomach and she rubbed at it. "I swear the baby has been playing kickball today."

Toni gave her a compassionate smile, experiencing the tiniest bit of envy. She'd always believed that one day she would have a family of her own; maybe two or three children. Stanley hadn't been excited about it. He'd been more interested in her keeping her figure. He'd even suggested that they adopt…in another few years. And he'd never once made love with her without wearing a condom. She had a feeling that he'd checked and double-checked every condom he used, determined to make sure there were no accidents.

Had he been that careful with the woman he'd started seeing on the side? Definitely a subject she didn't want to think about. If the other woman got pregnant, tough.

She shoved the distressing thoughts away. "Go home and put your feet up. Let your husband spoil you and make supper. Just relax." She'd already heard about how Ellen's husband watched over her almost to the point of driving her crazy. He massaged the woman's swollen feet each night. Definitely love. Something Toni was sure she'd never experience, because she wasn't going to allow another man anywhere close to her heart.

"Good advice, which I'm taking." Ellen turned to leave, stopping to say, "Oh, Chad buzzed me a couple of minutes ago. He said you can go to his office any time. He's ready now."

Toni watched the woman leave; didn't move even as she heard the front door lock. Her stomach fluttered with nerves. She'd been dreading this all day, particularly since the awful mistake she'd made earlier. If she were a real employee, she would probably be fired for it. How would her error affect this situation?

Chad glanced at the large regulator clock on the wall opposite his desk: 5:15. He'd told Ellen to send Toni up to his office and he'd heard the outer door closing as the receptionist left. He hadn't had any real plans for this meeting, other than making sure Toni was doing okay here. He was worried about her, and uncertain about how to help her with transitioning from a bad marriage and ugly divorce to life back in her hometown.

Another ten minutes passed. She was avoiding him. He didn't like the idea, but was wary about pressuring her. What had she thought about the flowers he'd gotten her in a spur-of-the-moment decision? Even his father had wondered, but he'd signed the card before hurrying off to appointments this morning. He didn't normally wrestle this much with decisions he made. He'd just wanted to do something nice for her. Maybe he'd overstepped some line that needed to be in place between them while she worked here.

Okay, she wasn't coming. He wasn't mad about it, disappointed. With a last glance at the paperwork he'd straightened on his desk, he started to get up. Then he heard footsteps slowly inching up the staircase, and relief filled him.

He concentrated on not staring at the doorway, not wanting to make her even more uncomfortable. He'd been uneasy all day. He'd been aware of her presence in the office from the minute she'd walked into the board meeting. Later, her soft laugh had drifted to him in the kitchen when he'd gone down for another cup of coffee. She and Ellen were getting along and enjoying each other. He'd worried at first that Ellen wouldn't be able to get past her hesitance at having the woman who had caused him injury working here. But Toni had won her over. Good.

The scent of Toni's soft, sensuous perfume drifted into his office on the breeze from the overhead fan. Everything in him knew the instant she stepped into the doorway. His immediate reaction surprised him, troubled him. Even during the flare up about the house the other day, he'd sensed something more than anger simmering between them. He hadn't wanted to think about that too much, still didn't want to.

When he thought he'd regained some control, he looked up. She stood stiffly; the color had drained from her creamy face, making the sprinkling of freckles on her perky nose stand out. Uncertainty flickered in her soft blue eyes. She worried the bottom corner of her lower lip, which had his control slipping again. Something about the action was so enticing, so sexy. *Don't go there.*

So he shifted his gaze to her long, wavy red hair. He'd been thinking about it ever since first seeing her the other day. Earlier she'd worn it pulled up in one of those banana clips women sometimes wore. Every time he'd seen her, he'd wanted to remove it and let that mass of soft curls fall freely over her shoulders. At some point in the afternoon she had let it down. Now it teased him. The musing about her hair didn't help his situation.

"I hope your first day here went all right." He slid the stacked papers in front of him back into the folder sitting next to the pile.

She took a step closer. "Except for that minor incident with the Claymore file," she said in a near whisper.

She'd somehow misunderstood Ellen's instructions and shredded a lot of the estate file's documents.

From his office, he'd overheard Ellen's panicked cries about the problem. He'd started down the stairs to find out what was happening, but had stopped to hear Toni's distressed sobs about being "so sorry."

When Ellen had calmed down and reassured her that the entire file was backed up in multiple places and that they could print out the documents again, he changed his direction and returned to his office. He'd been somewhat frustrated, but hadn't wanted to upset Toni further.

"You need to pay better attention to instructions," he said, knowing she expected him to say something. "That could have been a real disaster."

She nodded, her lower lip wobbling. "I'll do better, I promise."

Their gazes locked and he saw what looked like fear in her eyes. It sickened him. The young woman he'd once known wouldn't have reacted that way when chastised about something. She'd have thrust out her chin and challenged being told she'd done wrong. Just what had her ex-husband done to her?

"Are you in much pain?" she asked cautiously, pulling him from his distressed thoughts.

"Less now than last night. I'm healing all right."

She lowered her gaze, then looked up again. "Ellen ordered your new sign this afternoon. And she said you had already ordered a new iPad." She finally shoved out her chin, which he was pleased to see. "I'll be paying for both items, of course. And I'll need your medical bills as well."

He nodded, remembering the broken sign. He'd been stunned and a bit amazed at her obvious strength. As wrong as her actions had been, it gave him hope that the spirited woman in her would be resurfacing. That what her ex had done to her wouldn't be keeping her down forever.

"Not that I'm at all happy with what you did to the sign, I admit that was impressive. You just kicked it, right?" He offered a careful smile.

Her face flamed. "Karate classes."

Neither of them spoke for several minutes. He wasn't sure what to say, felt like he was walking on eggshells, like the saying went. She'd changed in so many ways; some good, some bad. She'd matured into a woman that had filled out in all of the right places. He liked the plumpness of her breasts pushing at the front of her silky white blouse. The black, pencil-styled skirt that ended several inches above her knees complimented shapely hips. And the red, thin-strapped stilettos were man-killers, making her legs appear long and tempting. His mind quickly envisioned her wearing only them and nothing else. Once more his body paid far too much attention to all of that.

"I wish everyone would stop being so careful around me," she said, the sadness in her tone pulling at him. She inched closer. "I behaved horribly and I know that."

"And you're paying for it."

"Financially, yes."

"By serving community service, too."

A spark of her familiar temper surfaced. "Yes. In the very place from my destroyed dreams."

He felt bad about that, but there was no going back. "You need to get over your disappointment about not being able to buy this house."

"But *I am* in the process of buying it." She blinked rapidly; tears shimmered in the sad eyes. "At least I thought I was. I'm so confused about where I stand, about where *you* stand. But I'll definitely be calling my realtor and demanding to know what exactly is going on."

He frowned. It was a situation that he needed to look into more. He and his father had thought the legal issues were being worked out, slowly. They'd temporarily rented the house and paid for remodeling on good faith until the sale was completed. Now what?

"We'll be calling our realtor as well."

She sniffled and made him forget the problem for now. He watched her draw in a breath and swallow hard. Once more, he wanted to go to her and pull her into his embrace, comfort her. It would be a bad idea, though.

"So much has happened to me. Too much." She swiped at her eyes. "Buying this house gave me something to focus on and look forward to. Now... now I'm feeling lost all over again."

He hated hearing the hurt in her tone and seeing the helpless slump to her shoulders. Bad idea or not, he stood and walked around the desk, needing to offer comfort in some way. He reached for her, barely remembering her previous reaction until it was too late.

Her eyes widened and she scuttled backward. "No! Don't touch me!"

Toni panicked. Instinctively she knew Chad didn't intend to harm her. But she couldn't help her reaction. She trembled, fought down the fear, and was miserable at the sight of him watching her in caution. She didn't want him to think she was a crazy woman, but it was hard to clarify what had happened.

As her breathing returned to almost normal, she looked at him, needing to explain a part of her problem. "You deserve to know why I reacted this way now…and the other day."

He shook his head, his eyes determined. "No. It's all right."

"No it isn't," she protested. She called on her limited inner strength to get through the explanation. "The last day Stanley and I were together was bad. As he was leaving the house for the office in the morning, I confronted him about a woman who'd called for him the day before. She hadn't told me her name and had laughed as she hung up. I'd worried about it all night. When I asked him who she was, he got mad and told me it wasn't any of my business."

Chad heaved an angry breath, but didn't say anything.

She was grateful for that and went back to the devastating moment, feeling sick inside. "I knew then. I knew that she was who he'd been seeing those nights he'd started staying away from home." She closed her eyes in shame, admitting quietly. "I was certain his cheating on me was my fault. That I'd not been woman enough for him, which is something he'd started mentioning…that I wasn't giving him the passion he needed anymore. He told me that I wasn't woman enough for him, or for any real man."

That had hurt almost more than any of the physical pain she'd suffered from him. She'd always done whatever he wanted, and he'd demanded a lot sometimes.

A tear slipped from one eye, both from the awful recollection and from knowing what a fool she'd been back then. "I had to do something to save my marriage. So I made him a special dinner that night, planned to seduce him somehow."

She glanced at Chad and found him rigid, his jaw tight. She looked away in embarrassment. Why was she telling him all of this? What would he think of her? She was a woman who hadn't been able to hang onto her husband.

Then she felt her anger returning. "The food was barely warm by the time Stanley got home from work. He didn't want to eat, but I insisted. I'd worked so hard on it. So he ate some of it, getting more irritated with me with every bite he swallowed."

She remembered seeing the annoyance in his expression. "Finally I gave up and stood to take the dishes to the kitchen. He got up, too, furious now that I was going to put the food away. Food he'd not wanted to eat."

"He'd been angry before, yelled at me, called me…called me awful things. But this was worse than ever before. He was so mad."

She pulled in a shaky breath, seeing the anger on his face in her mind's eye. "He grabbed me, forced me to drop the plate, which broke at my feet. That made him more upset. He took hold of both of my arms and shook me. His grip was so hard that he left bruises that lasted for days." She gulped down a lump of emotion. "Then he pushed me, hard. I fell and knocked my head on the table edge."

Chad cursed under his breath, "That sonofabitch."

Ignoring his statement, she looked miserably at him. "Like...like I pushed you." Tears blurred her vision at what she'd done, at the violence within her that had never been in her before Stanley.

Again, Chad grumbled in frustration.

She ignored him and went on, needing to get this out. "He looked in disgust at me lying there on the floor. Hatred, really. Then he walked out of the house without saying a word."

"He wasn't good enough for you, Toni," Chad protested. "The bastard."

For a second, she considered what he said and wanted to believe him, but there were still enough uncertain feelings within her to doubt herself.

"Had Beaton done that before? Hit you?" Chad asked through gritted teeth.

She blinked away the tears she refused to shed. "Just a couple of times, just slaps. But he apologized over and over after it happened each time. He promised it would never happen again. But it did. Only worse."

Chapter Five

Chad wanted to find the asshole and shove his hand right through his face. He'd hurt Toni in ways that caused soul deep pain as well as physical pain. Beaton had gotten away with it. He would no doubt do the same or worse to another woman someday. He understood that with Beaton family's influence in Denver and her being a mere small town woman who'd married well, she wouldn't have stood a chance trying to take him on in court about what he'd done. In his work, he ran into abusive cases far too many times. People who had been verbally or physically beaten too much either struggled to fight back or didn't do it at all.

Toni had chosen to protect herself as best she could; she'd sought the divorce and walked away from that life. Not necessarily whole, but she was getting better. He could see the ups and downs she suffered, and would probably suffer for a while. He hoped that she'd gotten a damn good settlement from the SOB.

He'd been quiet too long while he struggled with what he'd heard. She was observing him and he hated that she might wonder if he would ever treat her like that. He wouldn't. But how long would it take for her to get over the experience? How would she learn to trust a man again?

"You should never have gone through that alone." If her parents had known… If her brother had known… Nobody had. She'd been completely cut off from anyone who cared for her, even if it had been her own doing. But here in Petersville she did have her family to help her heal from those wounds. Whether she wanted it or not, she also had his support.

She shrugged at his comment, then continued with her distressing explanation. "I loved him, or thought I did. I was raised in a good home, with good people, with strong beliefs. As his wife, I felt it was my duty to do anything he wanted or expected of me." She closed her eyes for a second and drew in a breath, then blew it out. "Some things were unpleasant, really awful, but I…"

Her admission cut at him. He didn't want to even consider what the *unpleasant* things had been. She'd obviously put up with treatment that a woman shouldn't have to at the hands of a man far from worthy of her.

"He didn't love me, though. I don't think he really ever did."

Her voice had dropped so low he could barely hear her, but he felt the pain of her disillusionment. Again, he wanted to find Beaton and do some serious damage to him. He shoved the anger aside and said, "I would never treat a woman like that. Most men wouldn't."

She appeared to weigh what he'd said. Slowly she relaxed. "I don't think you would. You're nothing like Stanley. He was twisted in a way. I should have seen the signs earlier in him."

"You were young…"

Her eyes flashed with irritation. "I was stupid, too. I met a man who paid me such special attention, made me feel treasured. Powerful stuff for a naïve young woman." She shook her head, the long hair brushing her shoulders. "I was so determined to have my way, like always. I was sure my parents were wrong about him. I couldn't believe they didn't see how much he loved me."

She snorted in disgust. "Love! *Right.*"

It was the sad truth that she'd spent most of her youth and teen years set on having her own way. She'd pretty much been the living definition of *brat*. Her parents had been patient as saints a great deal of the time. They'd loved her so much; still did. How different her life would have turned out if he'd not been such a damn fool and taken too long to make his play for her. His life, too. Guilt weighed heavily on him. But there was nothing he could do to change how things had turned out for either of them.

She looked straight at him and said words that had to be hard to say. "They were right all along not to trust him."

He put out his good hand to her, held his breath, and waited to see if she would take it. He needed to pull her to him, wishing he could take some of her burden of emotional pain. He'd been hurt as well by someone he'd thought loved him, but he had enough inner strength left to share her suffering. He doubted she would take a chance with him and let him offer gentleness with no expectations.

She stared at his hand for a couple of long seconds before she stepped toward him. He held perfectly still in surprise, let her be in charge. She slid her small, soft hand against his much bigger one and ever so lightly curled her shaking fingers around his hand. Her effort humbled him.

"So many people have turned their backs on me. People I thought were my friends and that I could trust," she said in a near whisper. "I don't want to keep feeling frightened, distrustful. I want to believe in people again and in their goodness. I know most people aren't like Stanley or his awful family. But it's hard."

Although it was awkward with his casted arm, he moved her into his embrace as gently as he could. At first she stiffened, but then he felt her force herself to relax and he knew it cost her. The rightness of having her so close made him want more. He had been with other women, had thought he'd loved a couple, but his feelings for them were nothing compared to what he experienced being around Toni. She was a broken woman, but was determined to believe he wouldn't hurt her. He prayed he could give her what she needed to heal. Like her family, he wanted her to be happy again.

They stood together for several minutes, his injured arm cradled between them. He experienced a twinge of pain as she moved closer to him, but he chose to ignore it. This was too important. He would stand here until his legs went numb if that's what she needed him to do. She would make the next move.

Her heart pounded against him, the speed increasing the longer they stood there. Finally she moved back and looked up at him with wary eyes. "I'm sorry for what I did, all of it. For breaking your sign. For breaking your arm. For—"

"It'll be okay, Antoinette," he said, cutting her off. He couldn't help himself. He cupped her beautiful face with his good hand, gave her a second to shove him away or yell at him. He prayed she wouldn't.

She simply trembled and waited.

Need tore through him. *It's too soon. She's too fragile.*

When she didn't move, he took it as a precious sign and he gave in, lowering his head. Her sweet, floral scent sucked him in. He was desperate, but he would be careful with her. She deserved gentleness. Their lips met and he struggled for control again. *Gentle. God, be gentle.*

So good, so perfect, even if so light. The tender kiss lasted little more than an instant, but she didn't fight it. When she gave a soft moan that was enough to try his patience. His body hardened and pressed against her. He hoped it wouldn't frighten her, but he couldn't help the reaction.

She drew in a startled breath and stepped back. Her eyes were wide with a mixture of alarm and longing. Regret. Then she spun away and sped out of his office.

Well, hell.

***

What had she done? How could she have let Chad kiss her? Toni's heart raced as she hurried down the stairs, nearly falling in the high heels, but managing to catch herself on the railing at the last second.

"Toni, wait!" he called from the top of the stairs. "I'm sorry. I shouldn't have…"

Oddly, annoyance filled her. She didn't want his apology, not when everything in her wanted another kiss. A longer one, a more intense one. Uncomfortable with that knowledge, she couldn't face him. Yet she had to tell him the truth. "I'm not sorry."

"What did you say?"

He started down the stairs after her, but she rushed to snag her coat from the halltree, and then her purse from her small office. He stood tall and worried with a pinched brow in the foyer when she nearly ran into him. "Did you say you *weren't* sorry?" he asked, sounding disbelieving, hopeful.

She'd waited years for their first kiss, having thought about it a hundred times in her teen years. She'd never really believed it would happen. Now it had. But it had been short. Still, it was even better than she'd dreamed about. Just a simple taste and she longed for more. She wasn't a teenage girl with no control anymore. "It can't happen again, Chad. I mean it."

"Because we'll be working together?"

"Partly because of that." She began tugging her coat on, awkwardly, since she still had hold of her purse. He tried to help her, but she moved out of his reach and did it herself. "Mostly because…because I just can't."

His darkened blue eyes held such sadness that she had to look away. "It was just a spur of the moment thing. Nothing you need to worry about."

But she was worried. She'd felt his body's reaction to her, to the kiss. He was a virile man, a passionate one. She'd sensed that, knew how much he'd struggled to control himself.

"There was a time when I wanted you to see me as someone you could be attracted to. When I was young and ridiculously had a crush on you." She swallowed hard. "Too much has happened since then. To both of us."

Disappointment filled his striking face, sporting stitches and a bandage because of her. Yet he nodded agreement. "If things were different…"

"But they're not." She walked by him and out of the office, hoping he wouldn't try to stop her.

He didn't.

Good? Bad? The right decision. She wasn't ready for another relationship, probably wouldn't ever be. He might never be either. Her brother had told her the other day what had happened in Chad's marriage. His ex-wife had aborted their baby, one he hadn't even known about. The woman's cruelty sickened her.

***

It took Toni two days to recover from that modest embrace, the even simpler kiss, and the awkward conversation afterward. She had avoided Chad as much as possible the next day and he'd let her do that. She'd worked with Ellen and Ethan instead. As she struggled with the simplest duties, both had shown more patience than she deserved. Answering the phone for the firm wasn't something she enjoyed. Too many clients grew subtly hostile after she'd said her name, wanting to be passed on to whoever they'd called for rather than even share a mere comment about the nice weather with her. The act of bringing a cup of coffee to a client in a meeting hadn't been pleasant, either. So she'd grown quieter at the office and tried to become invisible.

That was changing as of today. She hoped. She had lectured herself about her behavior this morning in the shower. Her therapist would not have approved of her shifting back into the role of playing timid, as she'd settled into during her marriage. That wasn't *who* she was, at least not who she had been B.S.

Walking up the office steps, she smiled. *B.S. Before Stanley*. Or more commonly thought of as bullshit. In her situation and experience, they were interchangeable. She'd been here almost a week and those around her might not see the changes in her yet, but she did.

Each night she went to bed feeling like she'd accomplished something, even if her duties weren't huge things, just day-to-day stuff in an office. Each day she dealt with the unfriendly clients, maybe too cautiously at first, but she'd learned to take their behavior in stride. Best of all, her redheaded temper had not made another appearance since her unreasonable attack on the sign and on Chad. Once she was confident in herself again, she wanted to keep on controlling her temper. That quick flash of anger she'd been known for in her youth wasn't something she wanted back.

Her nightmarish dream about Stanley having rough sex with her had also not returned. Instead she replayed Chad's kiss. Except the kiss had become much hotter, more passionate. Her body ached with desire for him to come to her bed, or take her to his. Foolish wishes. He didn't need a woman with her kind of emotional baggage in his personal life. And she knew he had issues as well, according to her brother. She didn't think she could deal with more than she already was.

Yet the man was messing with her mind. Each day she'd come into the office there had been another rose added to the vase, until finally there had been a bigger vase set on her desk. There hadn't been any new notes. But she knew who the flowers were from. Curiously, she wondered if she'd find another rose today. A thought that made her smile and made her insides tingle.

"Thank God you're here!" Chad all but shrieked the instant she opened the outer door. "I can't handle this. I'm totally inept when it comes to the basic reception duties."

After closing the door, she hurried inside. He sat at Ellen's desk. His thick hair looked as if he'd run a hand through it many times already. His eyes appeared dazed; a bit unnerved, too. He looked…adorably sexy in a lost man kind of way. Warmth curled inside her.

"Where's Ellen?" She slipped off her coat and went back to hang it on the hall tree.

The wheels of Ellen's chair squeaked as they always did and she knew he'd gotten up. She hadn't even turned around before he was at her side. He still seemed paler than normal, edgy.

"Her water broke almost the instant she walked in the door earlier." His eyes widened and he looked shocked. "Dad took her to the hospital. Her husband is out of town, but he's coming back today. I was a real basket case in her time of need. Helpless. She made me sit down and put my head between my knees. Dad laughed at me the entire time he was taking charge of the situation."

Her lips twitched as he blurted out his explanation. Poor man. If he got this distraught at his secretary going into labor, she couldn't imagine what he'd be like if it was his own wife and child involved. The thought sobered her. She remembered the abortion, his ex-wife's betrayal. She wasn't the only with complicated emotional baggage.

"Should you go see her at the hospital? I can handle everything here," Toni offered, although her stomach tightened at the idea. Could she really do it? *Yes, I can.* "Trust me."

He hesitated and that made her slump her shoulders. He didn't think she could take care of things. Well, why would he? Still, the idea hurt her pride.

His hand settled gently on her arm and she flinched, but he kept his hand in place. "I don't doubt you, Antoinette."

She raised an eyebrow at his use of her real name, yet she didn't correct him. The way he said it in such a deep, soft tone made her stomach go all fluttery. But she wouldn't tell him that.

The corner of his mouth lifted and his color returned. "Not going to sass me about *Antoinette?*"

"I'm cutting you some slack, just this once." She glanced at where his hand still lay on her arm. After the initial shock of the action, she really didn't mind the light touch.

Unaware of her change in response, he released her and shifted uneasily. "Sorry. I know you don't like to be touched."

She didn't want to correct him, so she headed for Ellen's desk. "I've already filled in for her a few times when she went to see the doctor. I'm sure I can do her job. At least for…"

She stopped, faced him, and asked, "You *do* have a backup plan for while she's out on maternity leave, right?"

He sighed and scrubbed his hand through his hair, shaking his head. "I guess Dad and I were trying to pretend it wouldn't actually happen."

She rolled her eyes. "Seriously? You're two fairly intelligent people. I can't believe you weren't prepared for this moment."

His cell phone rang and he pulled it from his pocket, appearing relieved. In a matter of a minute, though, he looked disturbed before he hung up after saying, "I'll be there as quickly as I can."

"Is something wrong with Ellen? With the baby?" Toni asked in a rush, tense, worried about her new friend.

"That wasn't Dad." Chad moved toward the stairs to go up to his office, but changed his mind and turned back. His jaw was tight and a vein pulsed in his neck. "It was Crampton. He went out to check on Mrs. Harper, like he does regularly. She'd been beaten, slapped around." He cursed under his breath. "Low life bastard."

She knew Mrs. Harper. The woman had to be in her eighties, maybe nineties. "What bastard? Who would do such a thing? Did someone break in and try to rob her?"

Such fury flashed from Chad's eyes that she took several steps away. But she didn't fear him. She'd just never seen him so angry.

"Her no good great-grandson. Crampton found him rifling through her jewelry box." He cursed again. "The SOB has slapped her around before. She wouldn't admit it the last time it happened. But I'm going to make sure he answers for what he did this time."

Her heart raced, memories swarming over her. Bruised, dazed, shattered emotionally, she'd had no one to help her after Stanley's attack. She'd gotten herself to the emergency room to be checked out. The young doctor who'd looked at her had wanted to call the police, but she'd known that would have made it all worse. He'd wanted to call her family, a friend, anyone. She'd been too embarrassed and refused.

She was shaking, lost in her pain, when Chad stepped in front of her. Before she could stop him, he thumbed away tears she hadn't even known were streaming down her face. He looked so worried, and torn, too. He needed to go do whatever he could for the elderly woman. Yet she had a feeling he wouldn't leave if he thought she required him to be with her. She did, but how could she live with herself if she didn't make him go?

She pulled herself together and stepped back, forcing a wobbly smile. "I'm okay. I just had a bad flashback. But I'm all right."

"I'll call Crampton again, tell him…"

"No! I'll get myself under control," she protested. "You should focus on Mrs. Harper. She's lucky to have you wanting to help her. I didn't…" She clamped down on admitting that she hadn't had anyone when she needed assistance.

He ground his teeth, anger snapping in his gaze. "You should have had people to rely on. Damn. What you went through…what Beaton did…" He blew out a breath. "I hate it, Toni. I really hate it."

"Antoinette," she corrected, hoping to calm him down. What he said made her feel better.

He blinked and some of his anger faded. "I don't like leaving when you're upset." But he looked worried.

The office phone rang and they both glanced at where it sat on Ellen's desk. She took the call as a sign. "I'm fine, really. I have a moment every now and then, but I'm okay."

She walked with determination toward the desk. "Go. Do what you need to do and trust me to handle things here."

He hesitated, but when she picked up the receiver, he finally nodded. She waited for him to grab his coat from the hall tree, pull it on while sucking in a pain-filled breath from shoving his casted arm through the sleeve, and then walk out the door before she focused on the phone call. She prayed she could stand behind her word, that she could deal with calls from clients and whatever else would be necessary. But, truthfully, she was scared almost witless.

After she'd survived the first call, she went to her office and snagged the vase of roses. She smiled as she quickly counted them. Another new one. Red this time, full and beautiful. It made her wonder what the florist thought about Chad buying a new one each day.

Feeling good about the flowers, she carried the vase back to Ellen's desk. Since she was in a better mood, confident, she'd give Caruthers a call. She'd been trying to get hold of him for several days now, but he never answered...and he never called her back. Today would hopefully be the day they connected.

Chapter Six

By five o'clock and Toni could finally close the office, she wanted nothing more than to go home and collapse. At least this was the last day of the workweek. It had been wild ever since Chad had left. The small town's gossip vine had been active all day. Clients had called to find out what she'd heard about Ellen and her baby, but poor Ellen was still in labor. According to Ethan when he'd checked in with her, the younger woman was unfortunately one of those first time mothers who experienced long labors. But the doctor wasn't worried. Her husband was a bit nuts with the situation, as was her large family, who had insisted on staying at the hospital. Ethan had decided to stay there as well and help keep everyone as calm as possible. He was a good man. Widowed years ago, back when Chad was eight.

For the first time since she'd started work here, no one who called had made her uncomfortable. Some even knew what had taken Chad away from the office and his scheduled appointments. They'd acted concerned for the elderly woman and had no problem rescheduling their meetings with both Chad and Ethan. Basically, the day had gone far better than she'd thought it would.

Except for her family. Her mother had called to check on her several times. Her father had stopped by to make sure she was all right. Ted, too, had called and dropped in. While their concern felt good, she hated that they must think she was incapable of dealing with a job on her own. That depressed her. She wasn't looking forward to an evening being smothered by their good intentions; by their belief that she needed coddling.

She pulled the front door closed, locked it, and stood on the porch for a second. The air had turned colder and a bitter breeze whipped around her. Almost March and snow was still a possibility and she could almost feel it. What she really wanted was to go to her own home - not her parents' house - and curl up on a sofa with a glass of red wine and....

No, there wouldn't be any wine or alcohol of any kind involved in relaxing anymore. Her life with Stanley had meant attending far too many parties where the only drinks were alcoholic, or spending evenings with his friends and doing wine tastings. She'd discovered that she was susceptible to the lure of getting a buzz on. When the social experiences were difficult for her, she'd found surviving them easier with more and more alcohol.

The wind making her shiver, she squeezed her eyes shut as a still raw memory swept over her, one just over a year old. Although she had told Stanley she hadn't been feeling well all day, he had insisted they attend a Valentine's Day fundraiser ball. She'd been running a fever, but he just told her, "Tough it up. You're going."

They'd been arguing more and more by then, at least when he bothered to come home. She hadn't wanted to suffer another lecture on what was expected of her, so she went. Wine and heavily doused alcoholic punches were the only drinks available. He abandoned her from the moment they walked into the event. She wasn't up to making conversation with the few women who bothered to stop by and talk to her. Before she knew it, she'd started drinking; punch, wine, more punch. Her inhibitions loosened.

One of Stanley's business friends found her and they started talking, flirting. She didn't even really like the man all that much, but Stanley had been dancing with what seemed like every woman there...all but her. Suddenly she was getting dizzy, but happier. The man had touched the side of her face and smiled in temptation. And then she was kissing him.

In that second, Stanley had finally looked at her from across the room. She'd given him a sassy wave and all but draped herself over the other man. Stanley had stridden through the crowd. He'd grabbed her by the arm, hard, even though his friend had frowned at that. Her husband hadn't cared a bit what the other man thought. He'd dragged her from the party. He hadn't even stopped to get her coat.

The awful recollection made her tremble, feel his anger again. That had been another time he had physically abused her. The instant they entered their house he shook her so hard that she'd whimpered. He'd pushed her up the stairs to the bedroom and then he'd....

Oh God. She forced that awful recollection away. Never, ever did she want to think again about what he'd done to her. What she'd allowed him to do, because it had been easier than fighting him. Why hadn't she had the good sense to leave him the next day? Why had she still tried to save a marriage not worth saving?

Heart pounding, she opened her eyes and drew in a deep breath like her therapist had taught her to do. *"Take one day at a time. Put the bad memories aside. Start over. Make a new life. Don't let him have control over your life ever again."*

She was trying to do that. She'd gotten a divorce from the vile man. She'd moved back to the place she'd missed and was starting to make amends with her family. She had a job. Well, temporarily and only because she'd gotten in legal trouble. But she would get a real one as soon as she could. What she didn't have was a home of her own, yet. As much as she loved her parents and appreciated them taking her in again, she needed her own home and privacy.

The carriage house. She'd forgotten all about it, what with everything that had happened lately. It had been remodeled into an apartment. She'd paid a large down payment toward buying the property, all of it. Maybe the situation was a complicated mess at the moment, but Chad and his father were using the house for their office, for however long. She could certainly use the apartment for her temporary residence.

It still annoyed her that she hadn't been able to talk to Caruthers today, even though she'd left him message after message. Tomorrow. She'd talk to him tomorrow, or try to figure out another way to get in contact with him.

With that in mind and feeling better in anticipation of the apartment, she hurried around back, pulling out the key she'd already been given. It was time to check out her new home.

***

Chad sat across the desk from his friend in the Sheriff's office, waiting for Alex to finish his phone call to the hospital, checking on Alberta Harper. It had been a long day for both of them. Dealing with her difficult situation had taken a toll on everyone involved. She'd been horrified at the idea of Alex arresting her great-grandson for assault and battery. She'd tried to stop it out of love for the "poor, misunderstood boy." The "boy" was twenty-six and had always been into trouble of some kind. Chad had no use for him. He would do his best to see that he went away for a long time. This hadn't been his first brush with the law.

Alex looked exhausted from having to deal with Alberta, her great-grandson, his almost equally worthless father, and trying to explain the situation to Alberta's seventy-year-old son, who suffered from Alzheimer's disease. Plus, he'd had to transport her to the hospital in Topeka because she'd refused to go in an ambulance. Chad had gone with them. He'd tried to soothe her worries and used all of his persuasive skills to finally get her to agree to press charges.

He was mentally worn out. His arm hurt. Even the healing scratch on his face stung. He wanted to go home and crash, let his mind shut down, and slip into blessed sleep. At least he'd learned that Ellen had finally delivered a son about an hour ago. Which meant he and his father had to face the problem they'd foolishly put off handling: finding her replacement for the two months that she planned to take off for maternity leave.

Maybe Toni would...

Toni! Damn, he'd barely checked in with her all day. He thought about the antagonism she'd faced from some of their loyal clients and groaned. He'd called and talked to each one he'd learned had given her grief, and he hoped they hadn't made problems for her today. She wasn't the teenager many of them recalled who had been in and out of basically innocent trouble in the past. She deserved a break.

Alex hung up and heaved a weary sigh. "At least Alberta is calmer now, accepting that she needs to stay in the hospital for a few days."

"Alberta can't continue living on her own," Chad said, knowing there was a lot of work ahead for him in convincing her of that. "She's nearly blind. Frail. She's obviously unable to maintain her house any longer." He rubbed his stubbled jaw in frustration. "I can't believe no one else in town has seen how she lives, or at least tried to do something to help her."

He visualized what he and Alex had walked into. Her small house was on the outskirts of town, isolated, and looked almost normal from the street. Inside, though, there were piles of old newspapers, trash of all kinds, and a narrow pathway from room to room. A vacuum hadn't touched the place in who knew how long. Unsanitary and unsafe. Sadly, he'd seen similar living situations many other times in the homes of some of the elderly people he'd worked with.

"A problem for another day." Alex stood and rubbed at his eyes. The day had been a strain on him as well. "I'm done in. It's time I went home and let my deputy take over."

Chad got to his feet, studying his old friend. Alex had been quieter than normal today, withdrawn. He'd done his job, but something was bothering him. Now that he thought about it, he'd noticed a change in Alex lately. He'd just been too caught up in his own drama filled life to think about it. But something told him this wasn't the time to bring the matter up, either. Soon, though.

"I totally agree. My bed is calling me, too," he said instead. "Except I need to go lock up the office. I can't believe I hadn't thought to give Toni a key earlier." Or did she have one? Had the realtor given her keys and they just hadn't ever discussed the matter?

Alex met his gaze, concern in his expression. "She's calmed down? Not still behaving like a…well, wild woman?"

Chad stiffened his shoulders, feeling familiar irritation. "She had a bad moment. I wish everyone -including you - would stop focusing on that."

"Be careful, my friend," Alex said, looking even more worried. "From what Ted told me, she's got some serious emotional baggage. I know you had strong feelings for her in the past, but…"

"In the past, like you said. All I feel now is concern," he cut off the warning. He didn't want to think about his complicated feelings for her. Or the innocent kiss they'd shared. Or the way he basically obsessed every day about buying her a new rose because he wanted to make her happy.

One of Alex's reddish eyebrows lifted in doubt. "Just saying, is all."

With a curt nod, Chad turned to leave. He didn't want to get into any kind of argument with Alex. "I only want to help her get on with her life. Nothing more."

He wondered who he was trying to convince; himself or his friend. Sure, he felt sorry for her. She needed people at her back now, and helping wounded souls was what he did. That's all it was. Toni's psyche had been badly bruised. But he already had a full plate of elderly clients needing his assistance. He couldn't take on another problem. Yet he knew that's exactly what he was going to do, whether she wanted his help or not.

Again, he thought about that simple kiss, holding her in comfort. Both things he wanted to do again, as wrong as they were.

***

Toni fell in love with the apartment the second she walked inside and flipped on the pair of switches beside the door. A ceiling fan hummed lightly and the attached light illuminated what she could see of the small space. Most of the area was open concept, with the living room and kitchen together. She assumed a bathroom and one bedroom were through the doorway across the main area. The whole place had less square footage than the master suite she'd had in Denver. What made it feel perfect to her were the furnishings, pure casual. Not designer elegant. Not more for looks than comfort like the furniture in the Denver house.

She couldn't resist kicking off her heels and walking barefoot across the wooden floor to the thick, deep rose colored area rug. It had seen better days, but was far from worn out. She made her way to sink down onto the over-stuffed, pink floral sofa and sighed in pure pleasure. It, too, wasn't new by any means, but still in good shape, and cushioned a body just right. A pair of rose colored, stuffed and worn chairs sat one on each side of the sofa. A round, white distressed table was in the center of the tight space, with a light coating of dust. She could picture a few of her favorite magazines and a partially read book or two on it. And she could envision stretching out here to pick up one of those books to lose herself in the story. Reading had long been her escape from the reality of her marriage.

Maybe this wasn't what she'd pictured in her mind after she'd remodeled the big Victorian house. But it felt warm and comforting, at least for now. She would definitely move here as soon as she could gather up what she'd brought with her from her parents' house. The idea alone made her smile in anticipation.

Footsteps sounded outside the door she'd left open, snagging her attention. Someone was climbing the staircase.

Her heart raced and she sat up straighter, waiting. She was almost certain it was either Ethan or Chad. Would whoever it was be upset with her for being here? They wouldn't know she had a key to both this apartment and to the house because they'd never talked about it. A conversation that needed to happen soon.

"What are you doing in here?" Chad asked, a furrow marring his forehead, that sexy lock of hair curling downward. "How did you get in?"

He looked more curious than upset, so she relaxed. "I have a key. Actually, I had planned to live here while I worked on the main house."

His broad chest rose and fell with a heavy sigh beneath his leather jacket. "We need to discuss that mix-up, but not tonight. I'm beat. Tough day." He frowned at the furniture, glancing around. "I forgot how girly this all was."

That didn't keep him from stepping inside, closing the door, and walking over to drop into one of the chairs. Now that she studied him, she saw the lines of strain beneath his wearily lined face. His vivid blue eyes appeared tired, too; mirrored pain he seemed to be trying to hide.

"Did you get everything taken care of with Mrs. Harper?" Again, she felt empathy with the older woman. She knew how painful physically and emotionally it was to be slapped around; worse when it was done by someone close to you.

As if he'd read her thoughts, Chad leaned toward her, elbows on his knees, and met her gaze. "She'll be all right, like you. Even at her age, she has a lot of spirit." He chuckled and shook his head. The curl of dark hair that she found sexy seemed to irritate him and he pushed it away. "I need a haircut. One of these days when I have some spare time."

"I like it this way." Her face heated as she realized what she'd admitted. Too personal.

One side of his mouth tipped up with an intimation of amusement. "I like seeing your hair down."

She'd forgotten that she had pulled out the banana clip earlier. The instant her hair was not controlled, it became a mass of thick, reddish-blond waves that fell past her shoulders. It wasn't as wild as it had been when she was a young girl, when he'd....

"I miss the Little Orphan Annie hair," he teased with a smile.

He'd been the only one to ever call her that. A long ago memory. She chose not to go back to it. "Ellen had her baby. Did you hear about that?"

He sat back with a nod. "Dad told me. A boy. We're happy for her, her husband, too."

"Speaking of Ellen, did you have a chance to figure out a temporary replacement for her?" Her stomach fluttered with nerves. She wasn't sure if it had anything to do with having to work with someone else for the rest of her community service time, or if it was because she wanted to take care of the exhausted man in front of her. She'd never felt nurturing toward Stanley, so this was a new experience for her, and she wasn't sure how she felt about it.

He threaded a large hand through his hair, making that curl fall over his forehead again, making him frown. "I haven't had a second to discuss the matter with Dad today." He glanced at her, hope and a sense of helplessness in his expression. "I don't suppose you could..."

Once more she suffered from an awareness of her inadequacy, her incompetence. She admitted quietly, "You haven't seen my resume; not that I actually have one. I have *no* skills of any real value. Unless you count knowing how to serve on a committee or host a cocktail party."

His brow pinched. "Don't belittle yourself like that."

"It's not really belittling; it's speaking the truth." She jutted out her chin. "It has been a lot of years since I worked anywhere, and then it was fast food. Stanley insisted I not work. He wouldn't even let me go back to college." She slammed her mouth shut and looked away in embarrassment. She hadn't meant to blurt that out. A year into the marriage she'd decided she wanted to work on a degree in marketing. He'd hated the idea; actually laughed at it. Since then she hadn't even thought about the idea, not really.

She heard Chad mumble something under his breath and was certain it had to do with Stanley. He'd made it clear that he didn't think much of her ex, but then she didn't either.

"Look," she said going back to the subject at hand, "you've got my services for another three weeks. I'll do whatever I can, but my office skills are extremely limited."

Their gazes met and he nodded in understanding, although he didn't look happy about it. "All right. Dad and I will do some searching starting tomorrow. At least you can answer the phone and do the basics for now." He hesitated. "I assume you need to work. Have you thought about where you'll look for a job?"

Uncomfortable with baring even more of the awful truth about her life, she stood and walked over to the front window. She looked toward the big white house and felt the frustration and disappointment she'd been facing every day that she'd come to the office to work. "Originally, my plan was to focus on the Victorian and remodeling it into my home. Maybe making part of it into a bed and breakfast place. I wasn't sure about that."

She heard him get up to walk behind her. As he drew close, she felt the heat of him, drew in the scent of his after-shave; something sensual that made her pull in another deep breath. She tingled all over; more so in her woman's places. And that worried her. After what she'd gone through with Stanley, she hadn't believed she would ever be drawn to another man. But she'd always liked Chad, even when they argued in the past, even when he'd not seen her as girlfriend-worthy. And she'd liked his kiss, and the way he'd gently held her.

"I'll check into the legal situation. I'd like to see all the paperwork you have first." He touched her shoulder ever so gently. When she flinched, he drew his hand away. "Somehow we'll get this all worked out. I promise."

She faced him and hated that tears misted her eyes. "I trusted the realtor. Naïve, right? I'd trusted Stanley, too, and look how that worked out." She blinked and sniffed. "I know we have history, but it seems ages ago. I want to trust in you, but…it's hard to do. My instinctive trusts have failed me for the last six years."

"I know. God, just having to say that makes me sick, Antoinette." He held her gaze, frustration etched in his expression. "Believing someone shouldn't be so damn hard." Pain reflected in his eyes. He, too, had trusted someone he'd been married to and been betrayed.

She gave him a wobbly smile and dared to put her palm to the side of his face. The day's worth of bristles felt strange against her palm; strange but nice. "We've both got issues to deal with, difficult ones."

His vivid blue eyes narrowed. "You know about what happened with my ex-wife?" He stepped away, hands fisted at his sides. "Your brother, I suppose. Hell. That was personal stuff."

"It's not like Ted announced your secret to the world," she snapped. It angered her that he thought his "personal stuff" was more private than hers. She was sure that Ted had shared what little she'd told her family. And she'd told even more to Chad, though she still wondered why she'd done so. "Not like my marital issues were shared all over Denver."

She slammed her mouth shut, face heating at what she'd confessed.

His shoulders slumped and he calmed down. "Sorry. I shouldn't have reacted that way. It's just that what Sandy did is like a raw wound that continues to fester." He hesitated. "I'm not sure if I'll ever get over it." He pulled in a breath and blew it out. "You probably feel much the same way. I'm sorry for that, too."

Before she could respond, he reached for the door. "Not that we have much say in what you do here, but Dad and I won't have a problem with you moving into this apartment."

"Good, because I'm doing it tomorrow."

He smiled back at her. "That's my girl." He met her gaze. "Let me know if you need any help."

Chapter Seven

Chad sat in his regular booth in the Dine-In Café, nursing a cup of coffee, and waiting for Ted to arrive. Nearly every Saturday morning he met with Ted and Alex for breakfast and the chance to catch up on their lives. He'd almost called his friends to cancel, but Alex had called saying he couldn't make it this time. He'd sounded... Well, he wasn't sure exactly. Distracted. But he hadn't pressed his friend, and he'd decided to meet Alex after all.

He'd spent the night tossing and turning, reliving Sandy's devastating announcement when they'd left the courtroom following the finalization of their divorce. He knew the dream had been brought on by his conversation yesterday with Toni. Would he have had a son by now? A daughter?

He shoved the difficult reflections aside. There was no sense in torturing himself this way. He had to let it go and focus on his future. One without having the kind of marriage he'd long dreamed about. One without two or three children making him crazy at times, filling his heart with joy and love. While he still desired those things, he wasn't willing to risk the pain of being deceived again. *Toni wouldn't do that.*

The surprising thought shook him.

"Looks like you're mulling over some serious thoughts," Ted said, walking up and pulling Chad back to the present. He took off his bomber jacket and hung it on a post by the booth.

"So, are you helping your sister move today?" He didn't want to talk about what had depressed him so early in the day.

Ted slid onto the red vinyl seat opposite him at the classic Formica-topped table, shaking his head. "Toni packed up what little she'd brought with her last night. She had her car loaded and left the house before the folks even got around this morning."

Chad smiled, amused. "Another sign she's doing better. That stubborn independence she once had is returning." He was really glad to know it.

The middle-aged waitress they'd known for most of their lives walked over with a coffee pot. As she refilled Chad's cup and poured Ted's coffee, she glanced from Chad's casted forearm to his face. "You're looking better today." She studied him a second. "At least your stitches appear to be healing. But otherwise you look like hell. More trouble with little Miss…"

"I wish you all would stop thinking the worst of her," he snapped, glowering his annoyance. How many times since she'd been in town and acted out in frustration had he defended Toni? Too many. It wasn't right that he needed to do so. She deserved better than this treatment.

Elsie Mae's shoulders stiffened, but her expression softened. "You're right. Folks around town have been saying harsh things for too long. Me, too. And I'm regretting that."

Ted didn't appear happy about the discussion either, yet he visibly calmed down. "She's had a real rough time for the last few years. Not that I'm sharing any of it with anyone, or that I even know all of it. But I wish everyone would give her a chance. Toni isn't the same brat who left here. She's grown up. And she's hurting."

"Pastor Thomas has been telling people to stop judging her by the past. Reminding us that she'd been a teenager and she hadn't usually acted alone in the mischievous acts. Somehow everyone seems to forget that part." She sighed. "He's been reminding us not to cast stones, because no one is perfect." Her kind face looked contrite. "I spoke wrong and I truly am sorry."

Ted nodded, relaxed back into his seat. "Thanks for that. She's just been an easy target lately."

"That she has," she agreed. "I really do like her, always have. She was a good waitress here in high school."

"The regular?" She glanced between Ted and Chad, clearly wanting to drop the awkward subject.

When they agreed, she hurried off toward the kitchen.

"Elsie Mae was right about one thing, though. You look like hell today. What's up?"

Chad took another sip of coffee. His friend hadn't asked if Toni had anything to do with his exhausted, strained appearance, but he knew that was on his mind. His restless night mainly had been about Sandy. He'd also spent a great deal of the time worrying about Toni, as well as his growing attraction to her. All those years ago he'd been drawn to her youthful beauty. What guy wouldn't have been? That hadn't been all that had made him want her in his life. She'd been energetic, had a great sense of humor, and was challenging. He'd always enjoyed a good challenge. He was ready to have her taking him on again. Well, actually she had, about finding a temporary secretary.

But his problem with Toni went far deeper than dealing with the changes in her personality. He craved her. Bad enough that he physically ached whenever he was close to her. Something he sure couldn't admit to her brother.

"I've just got a lot on my mind. Mrs. Harper's situation. Needing to find a temporary secretary while Ellen is out for a couple of months." As Ted nodded in understanding, he lowered his voice and added, "Thinking about Sandy again, what she did. And your sister."

"What about Toni? Be honest, Chad. Is she more frustration at your office than helpful? I know she isn't really qualified for much of anything in the work place."

Irritated and reminded of his sister saying much the same thing, Chad grumbled, "She's doing her best."

One of Ted's eyebrows shot up at Chad's defensive tone. "Ah, so that's how it is."

"What are you talking about?" But he was afraid he didn't really want to know his friend's answer.

"You still have feelings for her, just as I mentioned the other day."

Chad gripped his coffee cup tighter. "I don't want to."

Ted looked sympathetic, his gaze concerned. "But you do. Be careful, buddy. I don't want to see you hurt again, and I don't want to see Toni hurt, either."

Exactly what he'd been thinking. Still, he worried that one or both of them would end up getting hurt.

***

It had been a long day, filled with ups and downs. Sleep had eluded Toni the night before since she'd been excited about moving into a place of her own. The condo apartment she'd had after moving out of the Denver home she'd shared with Stanley, while she'd waited to finalize the divorce, didn't count. In a way, she supposed, this small apartment shouldn't count either. This was temporary, too. But, somehow, moving here felt like she'd taken another big step in her recovery. A positive step in starting a future somewhere she wanted to be.

The downside came when she realized she was feeling lonely. Even though she'd wanted privacy, she missed her family. Not that they'd stayed away today. She smiled at the memory of her parents dropping by about an hour after she'd carried in her suitcases. They'd brought her favorite donuts from the town's one and only bakery. And they'd brought framed family photos, the last quilt her grandmother had made, and one of her mother's most prized teapots from her collection. Her mother was determined to make sure she knew how much they loved her. Her Dad hadn't said much the entire short time they'd visited. But she'd seen the worry in his eyes.

She glanced at the photos sitting on top of a small bookcase her brother had brought over in the afternoon. He, too, hadn't said much. He'd simply wanted to let her know he cared, that he would be there if and when she might need him. Again, she wondered why some woman looking for a good husband hadn't latched onto Ted. What had happened to Sarah? Or was it Suzanne? As soon as she got a better grip on her own life, she would sit down with him and have a real talk, about their lives as adults.

Her eyes stung with tears she'd been fighting all day. She'd been strong during her family's visits, determined to prove to them that she was fine. She was...and she wasn't. Her heart pinched in ache. What she needed was a hug. When was the last time anyone had hugged her? Her parents were too worried about doing or saying something wrong. Stanley certainly hadn't hugged her. The closest she'd come to it had been when Chad had given her a comforting embrace...and kissed her.

She sank down onto the sofa and sniffled. Then a tear slid down one cheek, and then another one down the other cheek. This was stupid, but what harm was there in having a good cry? Giving in, she began quietly sobbing. She needed to get these sad feelings out of her system.

Chad stood on the bottom step leading to Toni's apartment. The breeze around him was cold, a scent in the air hinted at rain coming, possibly snow. He shivered inside his leather coat, hesitating. He had debated for the last hour about coming here. Finally he'd known that he wouldn't be able to sleep tonight if he didn't check on her. No amount of telling himself that she was a grown woman who was perfectly capable of taking care of herself countered his need to see her in person.

He frowned. Should he have stopped to get her some flowers for her new home? She'd only made one small comment of thanks for the roses he'd gotten her, as if she was uncomfortable with the situation. But more than once he'd caught her bending over the vase and smelling the roses. And she'd set the bigger vase filled with probably too many flowers on Ellen's desk where she'd been working last. They meant something special to her, which made him pleased he'd gone to the trouble of buying them every day he could. He hadn't even really minded the teasing look the florist had given him each time.

Yes, he definitely should go get Toni more flowers. Before he could turn around, though, an odd sound caught his attention. Something from her apartment? He listened again and his gut tightened. *Sobbing. Damn.*

He sped up the stairs and knocked on the door. She'd probably be annoyed with him, not want to be disturbed. He should leave her alone, but he knocked again. When he didn't get a response, he considered pulling out his own key to the apartment. Maybe she was too upset to....

The door opened and Toni stood there in flannel pajamas sporting fanciful cows and looking sexy as hell. Except, her pretty face was covered in red blotches from crying; tears still wetting her cheeks. Her oh-so-kissable lips trembled. He stood frozen and suddenly unsure what to do.

It took a split second for her to throw herself at him. "Hug me," she demanded, sniffling. "I need a hug so bad."

He sucked in a flash of momentary pain, ignored it and snaked his arms around her, savoring the feel of her in his hold. He inhaled that now familiar, softly feminine floral scent. Along with the scent of pure Toni. He was lost in that moment.

Somehow they clung to each other and managed to move into the warmth of her apartment. He nudged the door closed with his hip. What he couldn't do was let her go.

She buried her face against his chest, her tears soaking his shirt. He didn't care. He ached for her, for whatever had brought her to this point. He kissed the top of her head and smoothed his good hand over her back. As he did, his body reacted to their closeness. He should release her, but he couldn't. When she'd pressed against him before, she'd turned and bolted away. Maybe she wouldn't notice the effect she had on him this time.

Neither spoke for several long minutes. Neither let go. His "problem" became much more of one.

"I'm so embarrassed," she whispered, easing back and dashing away her tears.

He missed the softness of her warm body against him. This shouldn't go any farther. Again, he considered leaving. Instead he gently tucked a strand of her wavy red-blond hair behind her ear. "Proving I'm the biggest jerk around, I want you, Antoinette. Desperately."

To his surprise, she gifted him with a wobbly smile, nodding at where the proof of his desire shoved at his jeans. "I can see that."

His face heated. "I'm sorry, not much control at the moment."

"I understand, similar problem." She glanced boldly at where her hardened nipples pushed at the front of her pajama top. "I want you, too. I suppose that makes me a jerkess, the feminine version of a jerk."

"What are we doing here?" he asked, worried, and at the same time relieved that she wasn't kicking him out on his ass, even if she should.

She shook her head, the long hair swaying over her slender shoulders. "Playing with fire?"

He wanted her somewhere - anywhere - stretched out before him. He wanted to... He struggled to slow whatever this was down, tame his wayward thoughts. "What were you crying about?"

Again, she smiled. "You're not asking *why* I threw myself at you?"

"I didn't mind that." The proof of his being okay with it was still rock hard.

She moved toward the sofa and sat down, curling her legs to the side. "I reached that point where I needed an old-fashioned crying jag." She shrugged. "Women need that once in a while. It calms us, believe it or not."

Since she didn't seem to mind that he was here, he eased out of his jacket and draped it over the back of one of the chairs. He took a tentative step closer. "Can I stay? At least for a little while."

"Sure. You can sit down." She worried her lower lip for a second. "I was feeling lonely."

He sat on the other chair and leaned toward her. "Hence the need for a hug."

"Who says 'hence' these days?" Her eyes danced with amusement. Gone was the sadness he'd first seen when she opened the door.

"I'm a lawyer. I say stuff like that on occasion." He relaxed into the chair and grinned. "Cow pajamas?"

Her chin thrust out. "You expected something slinky, something wicked and sexy when I'm alone?"

He sucked in a breath, immediately envisioning exactly that...and stripping it off her, too. He forced his gaze to the floor. "Flannel can be pretty sexy as well."

Toni's heart raced; flutters of longing spread through her. She couldn't remember the last time Stanley had found her sexy, or flirted with her in any manner. He'd been all about the "I want sex, I want it now, and I don't really care what you want." She'd felt less and less womanly. She'd just had something he'd wanted, not been someone he'd needed. And there were those hurtful words he'd said, *"You're not woman enough for any real man."*

Chad's arrival on her doorstep had surprised her. He'd come to see her at a time when she'd been seriously down. Being held in his arms had been so good; hugging him had been pretty fantastic, too. Even through the layer of thick coat she'd felt the solidness of his leanly muscled chest. And her body had responded to him. She ached with yearning for a man she'd desired for a lot of years. A man she had no business lusting after. Neither of them wanted another relationship; another chance at being hurt again.

"This is an incredibly bad idea..." She let the rest of the thought fade away. Would he understand? Would he run as fast as he could from the crazy woman?

His eyes darkened and his nostrils flared. "Really bad." Yet he stood and held out a hand to her.

She took it and let him help her to her feet. Then she pulled him with her to the small bedroom, nerves tangling inside her with each step. For a second she considered changing her mind. But she wanted this, ached for this. Still...

In the doorway, he turned her to face him, his look gentle and cautious. "We don't have to do this."

His concern soothed her anxiety. She could see the heat of his desire in those beautiful blue eyes. Yet he was willing to stop, to give her an out. If she did, it would cost him. Cost her, too.

She shook her head and disregarded the pounding of her heart, the fluttery feelings in her stomach. "Condom?" she asked to prove her determination to follow through with what she'd started.

The weariness in his expression had disappeared. "In my wallet." He pulled it from his back pocket and struggled to hold it with the fingers of his casted arm and his good hand.

She had to smile at his valiant effort and then took it from him. It only took a second to find the small foil package. She gave him back the wallet, still smiling. "Always prepared."

He appeared uncomfortable. "I was a Boy Scout. We learned to be prepared."

"I'm pretty sure carrying a condom wasn't in the handbook. Was it even discussed at meetings?" She raised an eyebrow at him in challenge.

He ignored her, stuffed the wallet in his pocket again, and unbuckled his belt, although the action was awkward. Frustration etched his face as he prepared to do more.

She'd caused his problem. Actually, both of his problems: the broken forearm and now the heaviness pushing at his jeans. The latter issue she didn't really feel bad about. It was time to help him out.

She handed him the condom. "How about you hold onto that and I handle this matter?"

His forehead creased in uncertainty, but he let her take charge. She went to work unbuttoning and then unzipping the jeans, concentrating on the mission. She couldn't look at his face and admitted quietly, "I've never undressed a man before."

"What?"

"I, uh… This is a first for me." When she hazarded a glance up, he looked at her in disbelief. For some reason, that rankled. "Stanley was *always* in control, including undressing when we…. Well, you know."

Sadly, she'd liked the way he'd taken charge. At least she had for a while. She'd only made one attempt to help him undress and that had not gone well. He'd not allowed it and warned her to never try again. She hadn't. She hadn't even been interested in doing so any time after that.

Chad blinked at Toni. The more he learned about her ex-husband, the more he wondered how she'd stayed with him for so long. Yet he did understand, because of the way she'd been raised. Marriages had ups and downs. His own parents had argued occasionally, at least what little he could remember, since his mother had died when he was eight. Like Toni, he'd been raised to believe that you were supposed to work things out, unless it became impossible. Which it had in her case. In his situation, too. For different reasons.

"The man was an idiot," he said in disgust and held her gaze. "Being stripped by a woman is…arousing all by itself."

Her pretty cheeks had turned pink, but her eyes sparked with appreciation. He wanted to ignore the casted arm and shove off his clothes. Then he wanted to rip away those silly cow pajamas. Instead he swore that he would find every last ounce of patience he had and let her do as much as she wanted. And, clearly, she'd decided to remove his clothes. *God, yes!*

She gifted him with an appreciative smile and returned to what she was doing. Except she stopped with her small fingers just inside the waistband of his jeans, an action that had his pulse racing and him wanting to yell "No!" Valiantly, he controlled himself.

"Can you toe off your shoes?" She looked at him in hope. "We should have started with that."

Immediately, as fast as he could, he did as she asked to each of his tennis shoes because she'd pulled her hands free. He desperately wanted to feel those soft fingers against his skin again. Just to be polite, he forced himself to say, "I can do this, really." But he didn't want to.

She shook her head and the long mane of hair brushed her delicate shoulders. "So can I, probably better at the moment."

She returned to her task, focused. When he sucked in his stomach, caught his breath, and prayed for strength to endure, she didn't even seem to notice. He was sweating by the time she wriggled his jeans down until he could step out of them.

As he straightened again, she stepped back to survey him inch by blessed inch. He felt a bit strange standing in front of her in white socks, boxers, and a chambray shirt with the long tails covering his butt. The shirtfront barely covered the tenting in front. Mainly, he felt pleased as hell that she observed him for so long that her eyes heated with longing.

He was overwhelmed by the urge to take this process much faster. But he managed to let her look her fill before she moved closer and reached for his shirt. He breathed raggedly all the while she undid each of the far too damn many buttons. He almost told her to just rip off the shirt. Finally she eased it from him, being careful of his cast. He wasn't sure he could continue being patient for her to take down his boxers.

"I can—"

"I'm doing this," she insisted, giving him the same stubborn look he remembered. She put her fingers in the waistband of his shorts and tugged them down and then off. She tossed them to his pile of clothes a few feet away.

His entire body pulsated with need. "Socks?" he squeaked out.

She gave him an impish grin. "I'm leaving them on. They're kind of sexy."

Her gaze moved lower and she smiled even more. "I think we should hurry the rest of this along, don't you?"

She wouldn't get an argument from him. Although he was more than ready for the next step, he was disappointed at how fast she removed her pajamas. He'd wanted to enjoy that stripping process. But the sight of her beyond perfect naked body wasn't a disappointment. She wasn't a tall woman, but her legs were toned and long. A curly patch of reddish hair covered the place he ached to dive inside. And her breasts, while not overly plump, were enough to please him.

How had he gotten so damn lucky? He'd dreamed of this moment for years. He had to control his needs, not push her. She'd been surprisingly aggressive so far. Still, he had to remember how she'd been emotionally damaged by the man who should have loved and treasured her. He had to let her lead the way in what happened between them. Even if it might kill him.

"Ready?" he asked as calmly as he could manage.

Toni couldn't believe what she'd done, what Chad had let her do. Stanley... *Stop it! Now!* She refused to think any more about her poor excuse for an ex-husband. There would be no more comparisons between the two men. Stanley wasn't worth another thought. Ever.

Her stomach quivered with nerves again. Yet she found the courage to nod toward the carefully made bed. Should she take the time to pull the quilt back? No!

"Lie down, right in the middle." Would he do it? Was she being too bossy? This was all so new to her. Exhilarating.

He gave her that sexy half-grin that made her hot all over, inside and out. "Yes, ma'am."

She watched the play of Chad's leg muscles and his taut ass as he walked to the side of the bed. *So very nice.* He'd been a jogger during his football days in high school and college. It appeared that he might still be one. She continued watching him as he sat down and then wiggled around until he was exactly where she'd directed him to go.

Her breasts felt swollen, aching. Between her legs she was throbbing, moisture building. When had she last been this excited about having sex? Years ago. When she'd been young and innocent.

Before she could come to her senses and change her mind, she put a knee on the end of the bed. Meeting Chad's steady gaze, she crawled toward him, like a cat inching forward. His lightly muscled chest rose and fell with deep breaths as he waited. His nostrils flared. And he gripped his shaft in his good hand. The small condom packet lay teasingly midst the spattering of dark hair low on his stomach. Was he going to let her put it on him? Her heart beat faster at the idea. Oh, she really wanted to do that.

Waiting for Toni to come to him was about the hardest thing Chad had ever done. He was tempted to ignore how badly it would hurt his injured arm if he grabbed her, rolled her to her back, and took over. Tempted, but he wouldn't do it. He sensed that she needed to do this her way, in her own time. He could give her this experience. The cost to his sanity was worth it. And, God help him, the sight of her crawling toward him was amazing.

"I'm going to need some help here." He could have ripped the packet open with his teeth and rolled it on by himself, but he thought maybe she wanted to do this part, too. So he picked up the condom and held it out to her, hoping she didn't notice the slight shaking of his fingers.

She blinked in surprise and straddled his legs, inching closer. The sensation of her soft skin rubbing against his hairy legs made him suck in a breath. He fought back another urge to take over. Then she smiled and took the foil package, using her small teeth to rip open the corner. Her eyes sparkled with pleasure as she did it, and his whole body heated observing her. It was a wonder he didn't spontaneously burst into flames.

Meeting his gaze, she blushed and admitted, "This is another first for me. I hope I can do this right."

She took hold of his length with one hand and began carefully rolling the condom over him with her other hand.

He sucked in air so deep he had to fight for another breath. Would he ever breathe normally again? "You're doing fine," he gritted out.

After a second, he came to his senses. What about her? He was ready to drive deep inside her, but was she ready for him? *Stupid, stupid, stupid.* He'd gotten caught up in the it-was-all-about-him thing. Still, he could smell her musky scent, which told him she was probably ready.

He glanced at her breasts so close and yet so far away. He wanted to put his mouth to them. But he decided that would happen at another time. Right now he had to have her riding him, and she needed this as well. He could see it in her fervent expression and in her darkened eyes.

She sat on her knees, straddling his thighs, her breasts rising and falling raggedly. He thought he saw signs of moisture between her legs, but he had to be sure. Trying to be careful and not frighten her, he reached toward her. "I need to see if...I need to make sure..." He was screwing this up.

A weak smile slid into place on her lovely face. "Oh, I'm ready, if that's what you're worried about." But she held herself almost rigidly in place. "If you have to check for yourself, go ahead."

Have to? Had Beaton insisted on checking her readiness? Had he given her any choices? Or had she just had to endure whatever the man had done? Disgusted by the situation, he pulled his arm back. If she said she was ready, he would take her word for it.

Again she surprised him by thrusting out her chin and grabbing for his arm. She pulled him toward her until his fingers touched the soft bush of hair. "My choice," she stated, as if she'd understood his thoughts.

He eased a finger gently inside her and she gave only a slight gasp at the invasion. When she didn't resist him, he eased a second finger inside. This time she drew in a breath and her eyes widened. He held his fingers still for her to adjust and then he moved them carefully, drew them almost out, and then pushed them in again.

Her body clamped around his fingers, pulsed against them. She looked down at him in wonder and he knew without her telling him that her SOB of an ex had not been gentle with her.

He wasn't sure how much more willpower he could muster to not move forward with what his body needed. "I..."

"Let's do this, okay?" she asked, suddenly pulling his fingers from her body and moving his arm away.

Toni almost cried at the ever so tender way Chad had checked to make sure that her body was wet enough to take him. The tightness of his jaw, the flare of his nostrils had shown her how hard he'd fought to go slowly. He'd been determined not to hurt her, which was a precious gift. But she was ready to take the next step.

She licked her lips, quivering with anticipation. He'd nodded at her and was going to let her continue doing whatever she needed. What a special man he was. How could his ex-wife have let him go? She must be as certifiably idiotic as Stanley.

She inched further up Chad's big, well-toned body until she rose up higher on her knees. Anticipation tore through her, yet she wasn't sure about this. Even with all of the romance novels she'd read, this was different. This was real. She hesitated, worrying her lower lip.

"Take your time," he said in a husky tone. "You're completely in charge."

Oh, how good that sounded. How powerful it made her feel. How thankful she felt that this wonderful man allowed her to have control. It brought tears to her eyes. But she could see how badly he needed her to move on, and she wanted that as well.

Her thighs shook from being spread apart for so long, for holding still. She lowered her body even more and took him barely inside her. And then more. And then she slid down his full length. It only hurt for a second as he filled her, then the sensation was spectacular. As if every tiny nerve ending in her body had come alive. She'd never felt anything like it.

Tears trickled down her cheeks and she closed her eyes. She wanted to relish this as long as she could. She might never have such an experience again.

"Damn, Toni! I'm hurting you." He curled toward her, his hands at her waist as he tried to pull her off of him.

She blinked at him and refused to be lifted away. Realizing he was reacting to her tears, she dashed at them and shook her head. "These are tears of pure pleasure, you silly man."

"What?" He stared at her in confusion.

"This has *never, ever* felt so wonderful." She smiled as he lie back down, watching her, still looking uncertain. "I was enjoying the moment. But now I'm really ready do this."

She didn't give him a chance to agree or disagree. She sat back, shifted his legs apart and held onto his knees while she watched his precious face. He appeared to be holding his breath, waiting for whatever would happen next. His beard-stubbled jaw was tense. Then she felt a slight movement inside her as he pulsed in impatience.

Spurred into action, she let her body's needs take over, let her instincts free.

He grunted, gaining her attention. His eyes blazed with need and he arched his hips upward, melding her to him.

Oh, God. How had she gone so long without feeling such pleasure? She resented Stanley even more for what he'd cheated her out of.

Stop! Hadn't she promised herself not to think about that ass again? Done. She was done with him forever.

Chad moved inside her and demanded her full attention.

She sucked in a shivery breath. *Yes! Yes, yes, yes!* More. She needed more. She rode him in desperation, her thoughts blurring. At the same time he met her every action.

She couldn't stop. He couldn't stop.

She gasped, panted. He grunted and his teeth clenched.

With a deep growl, he held her still and erupted inside her.

He was still holding his body up and rigid, when she screamed, "Chad! Oh, Chad!" Her own climax made her cry again, tears streaming down her face.

She was shuddering from the experience when he reached toward her and ever so gently thumbed away her tears. His voice was edged with concern as he questioned, "Tears of pleasure, right?"

All she could manage was a nod before she collapsed on top of him.

As she did so, she wondered how she could face him at work. How could they act normally around each other after this? Because this was a one-time-only thing. It had to be.

Chapter Eight

He hadn't seen Toni in a week. Chad hesitated on the porch before walking into the office. It hadn't been by choice; not a decision to avoid her, anyway. Work had gotten in the way. As soon as he'd gotten home that night after they'd made love over and over until they were both exhausted, he'd gotten a call from Alex. Alberta Harper had gone into a state of panic over the situation with her great-grandson. He'd wrestled the mounting problems ever since, in between having to handle issues in Topeka on another elder abuse case he'd been helping with for the last month. All of that had nothing to do with Toni.

Another situation had caught him by surprise. The board of attorneys that he worked with in Topeka wanted him to move his legal business to his office there full-time. He'd yet to discuss the matter with his father. It would also affect his relationship with Toni, if there really was one.

The front door was shoved open, startling him, and forcing him to take a quick step back. Toni came rushing out, looking frazzled. Her eyes glistened with tears. Seeing him, she flew at him. They would have tumbled down the steps if he hadn't managed to regain his footing at the last second.

"The deacons are talking about firing Dad," she blurted out, her voice echoing pain. "Because of me."

He hadn't heard anything about the matter and surely his father would have told him. The two men had been best friends for longer than Chad had been alive. "When did you hear about this?" And what could he do?

"Mom just called. She's more upset than I've ever heard her. Cursing. She *never* curses." Toni eased away, grimacing when she must have realized she had to be hurting him with his injured arm pressed between them. She didn't appear to notice that the cast had been removed. "Sorry. All I do is hurt you. Hurt everyone around me."

What else had happened while he'd been away? His father had said something about the temporary secretary they'd hired not being overly friendly with Toni. But he hadn't paid much attention to that, thinking the problem would work itself out. After all, Ellen had gotten past her initial resistance to her. He had a feeling there was more going on than that, though.

"I think you're overreacting to..."

"I'm acting crazy again. Is that what you think?" She shot him a disgusted look. "No matter how hard I try to get along here in this town, it's not working. People just can't forget my actions as a rebellious teenager." She nodded to his arm that he held gingerly against him. "Or what I did to you when I came back here."

Evidently he had some damage control to handle. He'd thought he had done that already. "We'll deal with this."

"It's not *your* problem. It's mine." Hurt settled in her eyes. "Besides, you've got your own life. Other people need you."

Irritation weaved its way into his mood. "You don't need me. Is that what you're saying?"

She glanced away. "I did."

"So that one night together cured whatever sexual ails you had? It was a wham-bam-thank-you, sir, thing." Even as he snapped out the words, he regretted them. Exhaustion evidently played havoc with his rationality.

Her eyes widened, misted for a second. Then she stiffened her shoulders. "If that's how you saw it, fine. I don't have time to even think about that now." She stepped around him. "I'm leaving. You can add another day to my schedule here or report me to the court. I really don't care."

"Where are you going?" he asked, feeling sheepish for his foolish comment, and worried.

She faced him at the bottom of the steps. "To butt heads with some stupid deacons."

"I'll go with you."

"No! I'll handle this myself." Frustration marred her expression. "It's time I fought my own battles here." She huffed. "But if you want to take on another of my battles - *our battle*, really, work on the problem with that realtor, Donald Caruthers. I put copies of all of my paperwork and communication with him on your desk." Her lips pursed in irritation and she shook her head. "I've been trying for the last two weeks to get in touch with him. Left messages that he doesn't return."

She was right about the issue. It was past time that he and his father looked into the situation. Something about the name wasn't right, though. Caruthers sounded correct, but he thought the man's first name was Harold. Maybe he was wrong. He'd have to double-check their paperwork.

"If you're sure you don't need me…" But she was already walking around the side of the house toward her car, he assumed.

Before he could follow after her, his father stepped outside onto the porch. "She's right, son. I think she needs to start facing the problems in town herself. We've already tried to establish that we're supporting her, just as Thomas has."

"Exactly what is going on at the church? They're really talking about firing him?" He couldn't believe it.

His father shook his head, concern and acceptance in his expression. "Actually, they're fighting hard to keep him there. Thomas handed in his resignation last night. Apparently Mary misunderstood, thinks he did it because they were harassing him."

Because of his daughter." Chad didn't need an answer; her father would do anything for his family. No doubt he'd finally had enough of the gossip about Toni from members of his church.

***

Toni parked her Mustang right in front of the First Baptist Church on Main Street. She refused to go to the parking lot on the side. She wanted everyone to see exactly who was here, and she knew there probably wasn't anyone in town who didn't know her flashy red car by now.

Snagging her purse, she pulled in an anxious breath, and climbed out of the warmth and into the bitterly cold wind. This was the second week in March and spring should be coming soon, but it didn't feel like it today. Yet as cold as she felt on the outside, she was burning hot on the inside. Furious. She hadn't been this mad in a long time. She hadn't even been this upset when her marriage had fallen apart and she'd faced lies upon lies in Denver society.

She marched up the dozen steps and jerked open one of the pair of thick wooden doors. She hadn't been inside this church in almost eight years; since going away to college. Mixed memories swam through her mind as she stepped inside and pulled the door closed. She'd grown up here, gotten into a lot of innocent mischief here with her friends. They'd stitched most of the choir robes closed one time, turned around all of the books in the library so the titles faced away. They'd...

"If you're looking for the Deacons' meeting, they're in the church lounge."

Jerked out of her musings, Toni glanced in surprise at the church secretary who had walked out of her nearby office. A gentle smile lit the much older woman's face. Berniece Chatterly had never had an unkind word for anybody, as far as Toni knew. And she'd always tried to calm down her father and the church leaders whenever she and her friends got into trouble. She had a kind soul.

Toni gave a curt nod of acknowledgment. "I can't let them treat him like this. I can't let them fire him."

"But..."

She didn't wait for any possible excuse Berniece might have for the idiocy of the situation. She strode briskly down the tiled hallway toward the lounge. With each step taken, she got madder and madder. How dare they do this to her father? This church was his life. He loved each and every one of his parishioners. He looked after them; he helped them however he could. No. This was *not* happening!

The door was shut and she heard voices inside, but she didn't waste time with knocking. She gripped the handle and opened the door, burst into the room. The dozen middle-aged and elderly Deacons she'd known for years gaped at her in surprise. Her father stood frowning by the window overlooking the back parking lot.

Without hesitation, she snapped, "You cannot fire my father! He's the best preacher in the whole Southern Baptist Convention."

"Toni," her father interrupted, sounding confused.

She glanced at him and focused on the men sitting around a large table. "He's also the most loving, most supportive father anyone could ever want. Believe me, I've caused him more headaches over the years than any person should ever have to suffer. I still do."

The men watched her, looking curious, including the three who had been in the meeting her first day working at Chad's office. She had to get through to them; had to make them see that, whatever her father might have done or said to support her, his job shouldn't be at risk because of it. She would do anything; even if she had to tell them about the humiliation that had been her life until recently.

"Antoinette," her father tried again.

Once more she didn't let him stop her. "I admit that I was an immature young woman when I left Petersville. I went against my parents and their wishes. Because I was certain they didn't know what they were talking about. They only saw that Stanley Beaton was much older than me. They didn't see how wonderfully he treated me at the time. I was a love-struck, blinkers-wearing twenty-one-year-old."

She closed her eyes for a second; swallowed hard. When she opened them again, her father had walked closer. She held him off with a hand. "No, Dad. You need to hear this. *They* need to hear this."

He started to speak, but didn't. His eyes held such worry and such love that she had to look away from him.

"They were so right to be wary of Stanley."

She looked at her feet and then up again. "He was an awful, awful man. But it took me a while to fully see that. By then he and his family had managed to change me into someone who would fit into *their* lifestyle."

She decided to let that go. It was time she took responsibility for what she'd allowed to happen. "I was young and in awe, foolishly blind. I didn't stop any of it. It's all on me."

Her father moved closer again, stopping when she shook her head.

This was the hard part, but she had to tell them. She had to tell her father what until now she'd only hinted at. "I'm embarrassed to admit that my ex-husband abused me."

It was as if they all sucked in a shocked breath at the same time.

Her face heated in shame.

A few of the men grumbled in outrage. And her father cursed.

That made her blink. She'd heard him get angry before, many times. But she'd never heard him utter a swearword of any kind. What had she done to her parents? First her mother and now her father were lowered to cursing; something neither of them believed in.

She'd gone this far and she needed to explain a bit more, so they might possibly understand what she'd gone through. "Mostly it was verbal abuse that I won't go into. No woman should ever be called such names; ordered around that way." She looked boldly at them. "I took it because I was determined to save my marriage, no matter how bad it was."

She drew in another breath, gripping the handle of her purse until her fingers ached. "Eventually, he started slapping me when he got angry with me. It didn't happen often." She hesitated, adding quietly "I struggled with that, even when he apologized afterwards. I'd promised to honor and obey him, love him, too. But there was very little of that left at that point."

The older men were looking uneasy; frowning, glancing between her and her father.

"The last time Stanley struck me was different," she admitted in a near whisper. "I couldn't take it any longer. There was no marriage to salvage."

Her father was at her side, trying to pull her into his embrace. Momentary panic made her resist, shove him away, and then freeze in horror at what she'd done. She saw the shock on the men's faces, on her father's.

She had to explain. "That's what happened with Chad. I still have trouble with being touched, especially by a man. I'm so sorry, Dad. So sorry."

He opened his arms to her and waited. She knew he wasn't judging her, just accepting and hoping.

After an awkward second, she stepped into his outstretched arms, dropping her purse and not caring. She slid her arms around him and let him hold her close. It felt so good. She'd needed this so badly.

"Oh, honey, it kills me what you went through," he said with calm gentleness. "I wish you had told us. We would have been there for you."

"I know, but I was determined to make it work," she whispered, fighting back tears. "I wanted the kind of marriage that you and Mom have."

She heard the other men getting to their feet. She worried that she still hadn't made them see that they couldn't fire her father. Turning her head to face them, she pleaded, "Don't take away his church, his life. If he said anything or did anything out of trying to defend me…"

The older man who had spoken with her at Chad's office looked straight at her. "We weren't firing him, Antoinette. We were doing our best to convince him to take back his resignation."

She gaped at her father. "You resigned?"

He looked uncertain. "I thought maybe you needed me right now more than my church does. If I can't be there for my own daughter when she's suffering, how can I help anyone else?"

"Oh, Daddy." She watched him smile at her childhood name for him. "I'm getting stronger every day. I'm moving past what happened. I came back here to find myself again, to live where people are good, where they care about each other."

She glanced at the men still watching and listening. "Even though sometimes a few people have trouble letting go of what happened when I was a teenager." She sighed. "Well, and what I did to Chad. It was a reaction, a final disappointment that broke me...for a moment. An incident that I deeply regret, and am paying for."

"Things will get better here," the Deacon leader stated firmly. "We'll make sure of that. And, for my part, I'm sorry for misjudging you." He offered a sympathetic look. "If my daughter had gone through what you did..."

She smiled through teary eyes. "Thank you for that." She gazed at her father and back to the men. "He'll be staying on as your minister," she stated, determined that would be true.

***

"Chad Anderson," he said into the phone; a bit distracted as he glanced up from the contract Toni had signed in connection to the house. No matter how many times he'd gone over it, everything appeared to be in order. Yet the contract he and his father had signed was as well. "Mr. Carter, I appreciate you calling me back."

"I got your message earlier and have to admit that I'm confused. You mentioned a problem with our family's property in Petersville, Kansas." The man sounded not only puzzled but also a little annoyed. "Exactly what do you have to do with the house?"

Definitely not a good sign. "I'm an attorney in the town and—"

The man sighed heavily. "That place has been a headache for the family for far too many years. None of us want it, but we can't seem to get rid of it. What sort of problem is there now with the house?"

"Do you know a Donald Caruthers? Or maybe a Harold Caruthers?" He tensed; almost certain he wasn't going to like the other man's answer.

"Caruthers?" Carter took a second. "There's a distant cousin by that name. Actually twins. But we haven't...." He grumbled under his breath. "What have they done this time?"

Chad groaned. Clearly this was yet another complicated situation that he would have to deal with. It had taken him several hours to sort through her paperwork and theirs. And then he'd tried to get in contact with both men by the phone numbers he'd found. Donald Caruthers' phone went straight to voicemail, which claimed the box was full. Harold Caruthers' phone was disconnected. It had taken a good hour of investigation and calling around to find the number for William Carter, the family's representative.

"Apparently they've gotten mixed up in some kind of real estate fraud concerning the property in Petersville." He felt stupid. Why hadn't either he or his father taken a much more in-depth look into what was happening with the sale? They'd both been busy with other things. And because this was a small town it just didn't seem likely that something like this would happen here.

"Fraud? Seriously? Over that wreck of a house?" Carter muttered again before saying, "This is going to be a long conversation, isn't it? I don't really have time for that right now. Can I call you back later today, maybe tomorrow?"

Chad didn't want to put this off longer than necessary, but he understood having other issues to take care of. His list of such matters was endlessly long. Besides, he needed to talk to his father. He would wait to talk to Toni until he knew the full situation.

"I'm scrambling right at the moment, too. And I need to discuss the problem with someone else involved on this end. How about we talk tomorrow, say late afternoon?"

They settled on a time and both disconnected. He scrubbed a hand through his hair. He really needed a haircut, but he didn't have any time for that luxury.

He glanced at the clock across the office. His stomach had been upset ever since talking to Toni, worried about her. He should have insisted on going with her, for his own sanity's sake. But his father was right in that she needed to handle the problem herself. It was important to be there for support when she needed it, not to smother her with his tendency to be over-protective at times.

***

After the eye-opening meeting with the Deacons, Toni went back to her parents' house at her father's request. As they drove separate cars into the driveway, her mother stepped out onto the front porch. The immediate smile warmed her and she was pretty sure that her father had called his wife on the way home. What exactly had he told her? She didn't appear to be frantic with concern, so Toni didn't think he'd told her about what he'd learned of her marital problems; of the abuse. She would have to tell her mother because she deserved to know. But she didn't particularly want to get into the miserable subject today. The chicken way out would be to let her father start the explanation with what little he knew. Yes, that wasn't the mature way to handle things. Still, in truth, maybe it would be for the best.

She was mulling that over as she climbed out of the Mustang. Her father met her and slung his arm around her shoulders in a supportive embrace; one that seemed to make the world all right. She'd felt ashamed by both what had happened to her and about not talking to them before. Now she knew they would get through this together. It was okay to lean on those who loved you and to listen to their caring support. If only she'd done that years ago.

"Thank you for coming to defend me," he said, giving her a light squeeze. He looked down at her. "Although I didn't need it. I can only imagine how hard that was for you to tell them your personal business."

He turned her gently to face him and his eyes glistened, while they shone with pride as well. "I wish we had known…what you were going through…what that monster did."

She swallowed against her own ragged emotions. It had been so long since things had been right between her and her parents; Ted, too. As awkward as everything was when she'd first arrived, she knew their relationship was on the mend. She'd been such a fool for allowing Stanley to keep them apart. No. He might have finagled the situation, but she'd been too weak willed to go against him. Pathetic. Never again would she let someone else manipulate her.

"I'm okay now, Dad. Really." She drew in a shaky breath and slid her arms around him for a real hug, which felt so good. After a second, she turned toward the house she'd grown up in and had fond memories of. Her mother watched them patiently, giving them whatever time they needed. Yet she knew her mother wanted a hug of her own.

She stepped away from her father and headed across the brown lawn showing early signs of green grass. Spring was on its way, even though today was rather cool. You could almost smell it in the air. Nature's world was coming back to life for another season. That's how she felt. Her new life was about to begin and she was more than ready for it. Physically she was fine. Emotionally she was doing better. There were still many issues to deal with: whatever was going on with the house purchase, finishing her community service, finding a focus for her life as her therapist had advised, and, hopefully, finding a job.

Then there was Chad. What was she going to do about him? She couldn't deny that their attraction to one another was a powerful force. And a complication for them both, too. They each had a whole lot of emotional baggage and were wary of another relationship. But being with him had been so good.

"What's on your mind?" her mother asked, meeting her at the top of the steps. She looked disappointed, as if she sensed that Toni was thinking about not going inside with her after all.

Her father moved behind her. "You're not staying, are you?"

She was torn between needing to sit down and have a long, difficult conversation with her parents, and her duties. Although she'd told Chad that she was taking the day off and he hadn't tried to stop her, she was letting him down. He'd gone to a lot of trouble on her behalf to arrange this community service. He'd been the injured party, but he'd ended up having her back. While it had bothered her to begin with, she actually liked working at his office. More so now that the clients didn't act as hostile toward her.

"As much as I'd like to stay, I can't. I need to get back to work." She glanced between her parents, hoping they understood.

"I'm sure Ethan and Chad won't mind if you take this one day off," her father said, but acceptance was in his gaze. He was still such a handsome man and the gray threading through his dark hair only added to that.

"You're right. They wouldn't have a problem with it, but *I* do. I owe them." She inched backward. "We can talk another time, all right?"

Her mother's smile warmed her. "We're proud of you, sweetheart. For taking responsibility. For…for just coming home to us."

"Go on, honey." Her father stepped beside her mother and put his arm around her shoulders, just as he'd done with her only minutes ago. He was a good man, the best. Like she'd told the Deacons.

As she settled into her car once more, she felt lighter; as if a weight had been lifted from her. It had. The dread of figuring out how to make peace with her family and share her horrible past had faded. They would listen, share her grief over the failed marriage to absolutely the wrong man, and they wouldn't judge her.

She was almost eager to get back to the office; even more excited to talk to Chad. He'd wanted to go with her, but she'd needed to go alone.

She'd had to stand up for her father and for herself. She had. She couldn't wait to tell him what she'd done.

With a wave to her parents, who were still on the porch watching her, she started the engine. Take one step at a time, her therapist had instructed. Today she felt like she'd taken much more than that. She had her life under control again. Well, sort of. She had to finish her community service, which was down to another fifteen workdays. But she no longer felt like she was floundering, uncertain what to do next. After the service, she would move on to her next step. It was good to be looking forward to something again.

Her thoughts were filled with possibilities during the short drive to the office. She should send for the few pieces of furniture that she'd kept in storage in Denver. They would be good in the apartment for now. She could start making some inquiries around town about a possible job; maybe as a waitress at the diner until she could figure out whether to work on a degree online, or what else she could do. The money didn't matter. What she needed was to keep busy and to ease her way back into the community. Maybe she would look up some old girlfriends here, if any of them would talk to her. She'd had to cut them off, too, when she'd cut off her family. More regrets.

Chad. She really wanted to run all of this by him. He was a patient listener. Maybe she could ask him to her apartment after work. She could fix dinner…maybe they could…. *Best not to go there*, she reminded herself. But, oh, it was so tempting.

She turned into the Victorian's driveway and drove around back to her usual spot. It was a relief to find Chad's car still here, having been afraid he might have gone off somewhere to a meeting or something else. When she glanced toward the big house, she spotted him at the open back door and looking in her direction. Had he been waiting for her? Had her father called him to let him know she was coming?

Anticipation spread through her.

Just as she pushed the driver's door open, her cell phone rang inside her purse on the passenger seat. She frowned in annoyance, reluctant to reach for it. As crazy as it was, she had a feeling that her good day was about to take a bad turn. She let the phone continue ringing. The caller could leave a message.

Chad walked toward her, warmth in his gaze, although she noted tension in his expression. Had something happened to Mrs. Harper? Or to Ellen or to her new baby?

The stupid phone stopped ringing and started up again as Chad stood beside the car.

"Aren't you going to answer it?" he asked, looking as frustrated as she was by the interruption. Looking like he wanted to kiss her, which she wouldn't have minded.

"I don't want to." But she pulled the phone from her purse anyway. "Hello."

The last person in the world she ever wanted to talk to again snarled, "We need to talk."

Chapter Nine

"No!" Toni snapped and ended the call abruptly.

Chad watched as her beautiful eyes narrowed in anger, as her face reddened in fury. Almost as quickly the color drained away and she swayed on her feet. *Good Lord, she's going to faint!*

He pulled her into his arms, ignoring the annoying problem of his still tender arm wrapped in an elastic bandage. "Don't pass out on me, Antoinette. Who was it?"

She pressed against him and drew in several breaths, her heart racing next to him. The knowledge that she felt safe with him was humbling. It took her a bit to calm down, but he would have held her as long as she needed him to. When she eased back, he experienced a sense of regret.

"Stanley," she said, looking panicked in spite of her sharp response to her ex-husband.

Rage seared through him. She'd been doing so well, putting the disastrous marriage behind her, and trying to settle into life here. How dare the bastard call her? Hadn't he hurt her enough? Chad tried to control his reaction for her sake. She was upset enough without him losing it.

Before either of them could say more, her phone began ringing again. He didn't take the chance of her answering once more, of it being that SOB calling back. He took the phone from her trembling hand and managed to thumb it off, then put it in his pants pocket.

"How about we go to your apartment? You need to sit down." He put his arm around her, closed her car door with his hip, and guided her to the carriage house.

She didn't resist his touching her, for which he was grateful. She'd come a long way since that day when she'd reached her breaking point in front of the office. Without speaking, she climbed the flight of outside steps with him. Her purse was still in the car so she didn't have her key, but he had one. He dug out his set of keys, glancing at her uncertainly. When she gave a weak smile, he opened the apartment door.

"I feel like such a wimp, letting him get to me again." She moved away and walked over to slump down on the sofa. "All it took was hearing his voice."

Chad closed the door and took a calming second before he faced her. "You're not a wimp. That scumbag should be locked up for what he did to you."

The color had returned to her face once more and she gave him a fragile smile. "I've come to realize that everything that happened wasn't *all* his fault."

He blinked at her. "What?"

She shrugged out of her coat and let it fall behind her. "I allowed it to happen, and not just because of the whole *love, honor, and obey* stuff. I was blinded by his charm, and his ease at throwing me apologies is not an excuse. I saw through them. But I wanted to believe in the magic of love too much. I wanted him to be the Prince Charming of my dreams. He wasn't. He'd never been that, not even when we started dating. I was just too determined to make him into it."

"You always were a romantic." He remembered how much she'd liked the Disney movies, especially the ones with happy endings for one couple or another. Ted had done his best to avoid them. *Beauty and the Beast* had been her favorite; The *Little Mermaid* was another one Chad knew she'd watched over and over. To his friend's disbelief, he had sat with her in the Thornton family room and watched both of them one day when she'd been miserable with the chicken pox. She'd been ten, he fifteen. He'd taken a lot of ribbing from Ted for doing it, but he'd done it anyway. Did she even remember that time?

She gave him an amused smile. "I don't watch Disney movies anymore. Well, not like I used to do."

He glanced at the coffee table and the thick paperback lying on top, a romance novel. After what she'd been through, it surprised him. "I would have expected you'd be reading a murder mystery or something dark."

She shrugged. "I still enjoy a good happy ending, particularly a story that pulls my heart strings. Just because there isn't such a thing in my life, doesn't mean I don't want it for others."

He understood why she felt that way, but it bothered him. "You shouldn't give up, Antoinette. Give yourself some time. Don't rule out having something special because of one jerk."

"Antoinette again?"

The name always slipped out when he felt emotional about her. It was special to him, but he didn't say anything.

She let it go and studied him. "What about you? I heard you tell Ted years ago that you wanted kids. You'd be a great father."

Standing behind one of the chairs opposite the sofa, he gripped the back with his good hand, tension spiraling through him. "I'm not sure about that. According to my ex, I'm too focused on my work." Just thinking about the cruel words Sandy had spoken that day ate at him. He still had trouble believing that she'd made the rash decision to have an abortion without even consulting him. He would never have allowed it, which was no doubt why she hadn't mentioned the pregnancy.

Toni's gaze met and held his, her expression gentle. "Like you advised me, don't give up. Maybe you're focused on your work a lot right now, but someday…"

"No," he cut her off, unwilling to even think about having a wife or children. "My life has gone another way and, for the most part, I'm happy."

"For the most part?" she questioned, refusing to let the subject go, reminding him of their disagreements in the past. She could be real stubborn. But so was he.

"I'm not good at relationships." He shook his head when she looked ready to protest. "I'm not. But I'm good at what I do. People need me, more and more all the time. There's Alberta and a dozen other elderly clients that I'm trying to help right now. You've seen my client list, my insane schedule."

He hesitated, wanting to talk about the Topeka matter with her, yet uncertain. They'd become friends. More than friends, but not really lovers, in spite of how they'd come together so explosively two weeks ago. He'd thought about that so many times. It had surprised him because of all she'd gone through. At the same time, he wanted to make love to her again. Desperately.

Doing his best to ignore the way his body had already started reacting to his desire, he decided talking was best. "The board of elder abuse attorneys I work with in Topeka have asked me to make my office in Topeka my main location."

Her eyes widened before what looked like disappointment slipped over her expression. She remained silent. That bothered him. "I'm only considering it at the moment. I haven't even discussed it with Dad yet."

"I'm sure he would hate to see you go." A forced smile slid into place. "If that's what would be best for your work, he would understand." She smoothed the sofa cushion beside her, avoiding meeting his gaze. "Would you move there? It would make sense, of course."

He hadn't thought that far ahead, but, yes, he would probably move there. The idea didn't excite him. He liked the small house he'd bought outside of town a few years back. Except that he'd begun to feel lonely there. Because he enjoyed being around Toni?

"Like I said, I'm still thinking about everything."

"I'd miss you," she said so quietly that he almost didn't hear her. She sounded as if his leaving was a done deal.

The admission surprised him, warmed him, too. More than his house, more than working with his father, he would miss her. She'd been back in town such a short time. He'd been upset with her leaving all those years ago, but now…. He looked forward to seeing her at the office, but that would only last a few more weeks.

"I haven't committed to that plan." He decided to change the subject. "How did it go at the church? Did you talk to the Deacons?"

She looked hesitant about shifting the conversational focus. Then she said, "Let's just say some of the ugly skeletons from my closet are out now."

Implying she'd talked about her marital problems. Damn, that had to have cost her. He walked to the sofa, sitting beside her, worried and proud at the same time. "You can be tough when you want to be."

She shrugged. "It's taken me hours of therapy sessions and earning a brown belt in karate, but, yes, I'm getting tough again."

He didn't want to think about *why* she'd had to toughen up again. He didn't want to think about his heavy workload or the problem about moving his practice.

"I know you didn't feel comfortable taking over as secretary while Ellen is on maternity leave. But would you consider staying on as our office assistant? After your community service ends." When she flinched, he wished he'd never mentioned that part.

She shook her head. "You don't need me there. And, if you leave, I'm sure your father doesn't need my help at all. Ellen is more than capable of handling everything." She looked at him directly. "Because of what I did you were forced to make a position for me. We both know that's the truth."

He couldn't deny it. "Yes, but—"

"No. As much as I haven't disliked the job after a rough start, I need to move on. I'm hoping someone in town will be willing to take a chance on me as an employee. Maybe the diner." Frustration lingered in her tone.

She got up to look out the window at the main house. "I'd hoped to spend most my time remodeling, but that goal has certainly changed. The house doesn't need me anymore," she added wistfully.

Guilt weighed on him, although the situation wasn't his fault. He hadn't known how much she wanted the place. He hadn't even known she would ever be coming back to Petersville. Still, he hated the slump to her shoulders, the sadness the emanated from her. The remodeling he and his father had done couldn't be undone.

"I'm sorry, Antoinette."

"It is what it is." She took a second and turned around.

He stood to finally remove his coat, then laid it over the back of the sofa. "I haven't had a chance to tell you I managed to get in touch with the Carter family representative."

"It's not good, is it?"

"Complicated." He blew out a breath of irritation. "William Carter had no idea that his cousins - Donald and Harold Caruthers, twins - were trying to sell the house. They have no right to do so. The family had pulled the listing from the real estate firm Harold worked with. They were considering just having the place torn down, and then try to sell the lot for some kind of commercial use."

She paled. "Torn down?" she questioned in disbelief mixed with horror.

He hated to do it, but she needed to know the rest of what he'd found out. "Before I called Carter, I tried to get hold of the Caruthers brothers. Harold's phone has been disconnected. Donald's phone just goes to voicemail, except the box is full, so you can't even leave a message."

Tears glistened in her eyes. "I...I should have known there was more of a problem than Donald Caruthers said." She shook her head. "I tried to get in touch with him, too. I left message after message, which were never returned."

Meeting his gaze, she said in defeat, "So not only I have lost a considerable amount of money, but also the house would never have been mine."

"Ours, either," he admitted. He still couldn't believe neither he nor his father had pushed on the matter more. All the money they'd spent remodeling… "But this isn't over."

A faint hint of hope crept into her eyes. "It's not?"

He walked toward her, remembering more of the discussion he'd had with Carter. "I had a long talk with Carter. He's agreed to sell the house. He's actually relieved to do so. He'll get the last signature needed and then get the title cleared for the sale."

"That's good, right?"

"Yes, in a way." There was more she needed to know. "He's going to try to find the Caruthers brothers and have the family's lawyer file charges against them. But, Antoniette, I doubt either of us will see the money we paid as down payments again." Which really angered him. Yet they'd all been too naïve about the situation and now they were learning an expensive, painful lesson.

She looked sad again, but accepting. "The family will sell the house to you and your father. You've already spent a lot of money on the remodeling." As he nodded, she added, "I guess I'll need to look for another place to live as soon as I can."

"I'm sorry." He hated the way the situation had worked out, but he and his father had made a serious investment. When he'd told Carter about what they'd done, the man had immediately agreed that they had more of a right to the house than Toni did. Good for them; bad for her.

"You can live here in the carriage house apartment as long as you want." He knew it was a small offer, but he hoped she would accept it. He didn't want to see her move out. If she wasn't going to continue working for them, at least he could see her when she came home. He could watch over her.

"That's kind of you, but…" Those beautiful eyes held tears once again.

He had to go to her, hold her, and somehow comfort her. She didn't resist when he put his arms around her. She buried her head against his chest, sliding her arms around him as well.

The scent of her softly enticing perfume drifted over him. As with each time he held her, she felt so right in his embrace. He stroked her back. "If I could—"

"What's done is done." She eased away to look up at him. The defeat in her that he'd witnessed and that had torn at him seemed to be gone. "I'll be all right. But I will take you up on staying here a while longer."

Relief spread through him and he smiled gently. "As long as you like."

"I'll need to pay rent, of course."

"No!" he countered, knowing his father wouldn't want it, either.

She smiled finally. "We'll discuss it later."

He would avoid the subject. What he couldn't continue to avoid at the moment was how much he wanted her. He needed to be with her as much as he needed his next breath. His erection pressed between them and he was certain she felt it.

"I..." He glanced toward her bedroom and back at her curious expression. "Can I..." He couldn't finish the sentence. His physical longings were not her problem. Another man had already used her for his personal satisfaction. He couldn't do it. And he had nothing to offer her besides good sex. He'd been truthful when he'd told her relationships were not something he was good at. She deserved someone in her life who could give so much more than he was capable of.

"How about we not analyze this to death?" She looked at him as if she'd read his thoughts. "Neither of us is ready to take on something complicated."

"I wish..." He wished things were different for both of them. But this was their reality.

She shook her head. "Not now." She rubbed his back, moved even closer to him. "How about we forget all the problems for a while? How about instead we..." She gave him a tempting smile.

His heart raced with anticipation. "The cast is gone, but...well, I'm still not completely healed." He'd almost forgotten about his injured and still weak arm until he realized it would still be a problem for him.

"We'll figure something out." She released him and then took hold of his good arm and tugged him with her toward the bedroom.

Even though she'd do this, Toni was panicky. Their first time together had been intense, which had surprised her. She hadn't thought about wanting anything to do with having sex after how Stanley had treated her. Yet it had been so different from her other experiences. Chad had let her be in charge. How many times had she thought about what they'd done since then? A lot.

Still, as she led him to her bedroom and the neatly made bed, nerves fluttered in her stomach. Could she really do this?

"We don't have to…" he said as she released him just inside the room.

She studied him for just a second. Everything about him was more than ready. His vivid blue eyes had darkened to almost navy. His jaw was tense and his nostrils flared as he drew in a deep breath. And when she glanced lower, she saw the thick erection she had felt between them pushing at his slacks. It made her swallow anxiously. He was so big, but she'd had no problem taking him inside her the last time.

"I should probably go," he suggested, though he didn't look like that was what he wanted to do.

"No. I want to do this. Really." She shoved away her concern. This man would never hurt her, she knew that. He continued to look uncertain until she pulled her sweater over her head. His eyes widened as he focused on her breasts, which made her nipples harden beneath the lacy bra. She felt moisture between her legs and soaking her panties. She ached for him.

She kicked off her shoes, then stripped off her jeans and socks. Standing there in only her bra and bikini panties, she felt apprehensive. But she wouldn't back down now. "Maybe you can…"

He took the hint and removed his clothes in probably record time, even with his bad arm. They fell scattered to the floor around him, much as hers had. "I want this more than you can imagine."

With a smile, she nodded at his shaft, thick and long. "Oh, I can imagine."

Frustration filled his expression. "As much as I want to lay you down, stretch over you, it's not possible." He glanced at his bad arm.

"You want to be in charge this time," she said in understanding. She actually wanted that, too. But they would have to do things another way. "We can do this."

She slipped out of her panties and removed her bra, throwing them aside. She knew a way he could be in control. With Stanley, she'd hated it. Because he'd taken her in both places, and she'd whimpered with the embarrassing invasion to her private place. But this was Chad. She trusted him with her body, and she was beginning to trust him with her heart.

Decision made, she went to the side of the bed. "I know a way."

He didn't move. So she went to side of the bed, braced her arms, and thrust out her bare bottom. Sensing him watching her, she spread her legs apart, giving him a view of her that made her a bit uncomfortable.

This is Chad. Relax. Her pulse raced and she fought down the compulsion to change her mind. It would be okay, with him.

Finally he eased behind her. When she peeked back at him, she saw that he'd retrieved a condom from somewhere, probably from his wallet. He rolled it on, breathing hard as she observed him. She was trembling with need, so desperately ready.

She should look away, but she couldn't. As she waited, he slid his free hand between her legs. An instant later he pulled it away, grinning with pleasure at the wetness coating his fingers. Why wasn't she embarrassed? Why did just seeing the glistening on his fingers make her desire him all the more?

"You're taking so long," she said breathlessly, frowning.

"I guess it's time to get started." He stroked his thick shaft while she shivered with anticipation. Their gazes met and he gave a wicked grin. "Thank you for letting me do this."

He stroked himself again, then guided the cock until it touched her pulsing, swollen lips. The sight was exciting to watch, but she had to turn her head away. She didn't want him to see how badly she wanted him. It would be there in her eyes, she was certain of that. She braced herself mentally and physically. And waited.

But he didn't keep her in suspense for more than a second. He gripped her hips with his big hands and the elastic bandage rubbed lightly against her. She barely had time to think about it before he drove deep inside her.

"Ohhh. Oh my," she gasped at the fullness.

"Are you all right?" he asked in concern. He held still in her body and she quickly adjusted to the thick invasion.

She pressed backward and his balls met her bottom. She shivered, longing for more.

"I take that for a 'yes.'" He pulled nearly out as she moaned in disgruntlement. He chuckled and thrust deep once more. "Demanding woman, aren't you?"

Every inch of him smoothed against her sensitized skin, rubbed places inside her in such a delicious way. But a demanding woman? It had been a long time since she wanted a man to have his way with her. Stanley's way had never been enjoyable, at least not for her. A thought which annoyed her. Stanley was in her past. Chad just might be her future. An idea that worried her.

Enough thinking about that! "How about speeding it up a little?"

she beseeched, quivering all over.

"Yes, ma'am." He began driving back and forth as she'd requested. His grip on her hips tightened and she heard his heavy breathing.

A part of her braced for roughness, for his undeniable power over her. *Not Stanley. Remember that.*

He eased back on the rhythm, moved more gently. "I want this to be good for you, Antoinette."

She could sense how much this slowing down was costing him and that knowledge endeared him to her even more. He wanted to make her climax first. Another special gift from him. The notion, along with the steady drive in and out, touching the most intimate part of her, had her panting. She squeezed her eyes shut as the sensations built.

"You're almost there." As if understanding exactly what she needed, he thrust a final time deep and stopped moving.

She flew apart, crying out in ecstasy. Her head dropped to the quilt as she sucked in calmative breaths. She'd climaxed repeatedly their last time together. He'd been determined for that to happen. But this...

He held still behind her with his shaft buried deep inside her. "Let me know when you're ready," he gritted out.

She was having trouble focusing again, but when she started to speak, he suddenly tensed.

"Did you hear something?" he asked gruffly.

"No." She kept her head down, wanting him to drive her out of her mind once more.

He didn't move.

Then she heard something, too. Was someone climbing the outside stairs? Had they locked the door? Oh, God, don't let anyone...

Chapter Ten

"The door," Toni gasped. "We didn't lock it."

Damn, she was right. He held still as footsteps seemed to stop at the top of the landing. Whoever was about to interrupt his precious time with Toni was not going to find them like this. He pulled out of her warm body with great regret and straightened. He looked for his clothes, which were mixed up with hers a good eight feet or more away.

Before he could do more than turn around, the front door burst open, banging against the wall. "Where the hell are you, Toni?"

"Stanley?" she whispered in horror.

Fury stiffened Chad's back. In the next breath, her ex-husband stormed into the bedroom doorway.

"Get the hell out here!" he snarled.

Instead, Beaton barely gave him a glance and focused on Toni. Chad knew that she hadn't moved, clearly shocked by what was happening. It outraged him that this scumbag was seeing her in such a private position.

Eyes narrowed in disgust, Beaton commanded, "Get up, you slut!" He stepped into the room. "I've come to take you home where you belong."

Chad growled and strode toward the scowling man. Beaton's eyes didn't look right, something was definitely off with him. His clothes were wrinkled, too. His hair mussed and appearing greasy. He was far from the man always seen in various media as Mr. GQ. Unstable. Dangerous. Had he been drinking? Was he on some kind of drugs?

Behind him, he heard Toni scrambling to stand. Her clothes were too far away for her to reach, lying on the floor between him and Beaton. There was a small rocker by the window near the bed and he remembered seeing an afghan on it.

He faced her for an instant, nodding at the rocker. "The afghan," he directed.

To his relief, she snatched it up and drew it around her. She started moving toward him, but he shook his head. "Stay back."

Another sound outside caught Chad's attention and he turned back to face Beaton. As he did, the man's closed fist plowed into his jaw. Unable to catch himself, he stumbled backward and ended up sitting on the end of the bed. He wiggled his jaw with his good hand. Not broken, but he knew it would hurt like the devil later.

The footsteps he'd heard seconds ago hurried closer and Chad knew whoever it was had entered the apartment. *Shit!* He was bare-assed naked, but he was more concerned about Toni. She would be mortified.

As he stood, she rushed past him straight toward Beaton. "What do you think you're doing? How dare you…"

He cut her off by grabbing her arm and pulling her toward him. He slapped her with his other hand. "You're coming with me."

She hissed in pain. "You're crazy!" She jabbed upward at his chin. As he lost his tight hold for an instant, she jerked free.

Chad moved behind her at the same time her father and Alex strode into the room. Both men looked angry but uncertain how to proceed. Her father studied Chad's nakedness, yet he didn't say a word. What could he say? His daughter was an adult and she stood wearing only an afghan in front of her fuming mad ex-husband. It was obvious what they'd been doing. He hated that what had been something private between them wasn't any longer.

Beaton took advantage of everyone's silence and discomfort. He reached for Toni again. But she leaned backward, arms crossed over her chest, and shot her bare foot right into his balls. He dropped to his knees, cupping himself, breathing raggedly, and glaring murderously at her.

Chad winced, as did her father and Alex. Although furious with Beaton, Chad allowed him a couple of seconds to deal with what had to be agonizing pain. Then he moved around Toni at the same time the other men did. "You sonofabitch," he growled. "You don't belong here or anywhere near Toni."

His eyes watering even as anger filled them, Beaton snarled, "She's my wife. I came to take her back with me." He glowered at her, spat out, "Cuckolding me. You're going to pay for that."

To everyone's surprise, she stepped to Chad's side and looked down at her not quite stable ex-husband. "I. Am. Not. Your. Wife." she said carefully. "You bastard."

Beaton struggled to his feet, his face beet red. "I'll teach you to talk badly to me." He looked ready to slap her again.

Not happening. Chad shifted her to the side, stepped in front of the demented man, and snapped, "You're *never* coming anywhere near her again. She's too good for you. Always has been, you lying, cheating SOB."

Beaton snorted. "So what if I did? A man has needs and when his wife…"

Her father moved in front of him and punched him in the mouth, blood immediately trickling out of the corner. The reverend stepped backward, shook his hand against the pain he no doubt felt. But as Beaton gaped in shock and dashed away the blood, her father looked proud of himself.

"Daddy!" Toni gasped, obviously as surprised as the rest of them at what he'd done.

All her father said was as he looked at Chad, "Think you could put on some pants."

Before Beaton could even think about moving, Alex was behind him. He jerked the man's arms backward and clamped handcuffs on his wrists. "You're under arrest."

"What the hell for? I'm just a man trying to get his wife back. His whoring wife."

"Take him away," Chad ordered, glaring at the man, fighting his need to thrust his own fist into his face. "Lock him up for every count you can think of. And we're filing a restraining order immediately."

When he looked at Toni he found her cheeks flaming with embarrassment now that the situation was resolved. Her father tried not to look at him. She handed him his slacks that she'd managed to find. But she pulled in a breath and eased in front of him so he would be at least partially hidden as he dressed.

Alex forced Beaton out of the room, but stopped to meet Chad's gaze. He winked and gave a small smile. His friend wasn't going to let him forget how they'd found him. And he'd want an explanation for how he'd ended up in Toni's bed. What he didn't know - would never know- was that he'd been in her bed before.

"Well, I guess I'll go with them," her father said, sounding awkward. He studied Chad for a second, again not mentioning about finding him naked and his daughter wrapped in an afghan. "Don't hurt her." With that he walked out of the room.

***

Toni couldn't move from the middle of the bedroom as her father, the sheriff, and her horrible ex-husband went to leave the apartment. Chad gave her a reassuring glance before following them into the living room. She heard his deep-timbered voice as he was all business. He would get a restraining order as soon as possible and he would do anything else necessary to keep Stanley in jail.

Stanley in jail. Locked away. Finally. Still, it was hard to believe.

"Whatever charges you try to file against me won't stick," Stanley growled in ferocity. "I've got more power, more connections with the 'right' people than you can imagine."

He did, too. So much that no one had ever believed her, except her divorce lawyer. Their friends and his family were fully on his side. He was the poor husband with the unworthy wife. But she'd gotten the divorce and he'd been forced to put five million dollars in a bank account her lawyer had helped her get set up. *Five million dollars.* It had seemed surreal. As did this humiliating incident. But *why* had he come here? What did he really want of her? The money back? So not happening!

"*Your power and your connections* aren't worth a damn here. You're going to sit in my jail until you go before the judge," Alex countered, anger lacing his words. This was not the gentle giant most knew and loved. This was a hard man, not to be pushed. "And I'm going to take my sweet time in seeing that happen. At least 48 hours."

"This is all bull shit," Stanley challenged. "I'll have your badge. I'll have you disbarred."

She sensed that he must be looking directly at Chad, which infuriated her. Putting aside her embarrassment, she strode into the living room, ready to defend her friend and her lover.

Immediately Stanley sneered at her. "You'd better stop this before it goes too far," he warned, his red-rimmed eyes hard. There was definitely something wrong with him.

What had she ever seen in him? She'd been blinded by youthful desire for more of anything. But she wasn't blinded by that any more.

She marched next to Chad and hissed at Stanley, "*You* went too far. *You* more than crossed the line between what is right and what is wrong."

His face reddened in anger, and he puffed up his slim form, ready to verbally assault her. She'd seen this expression many times before. Back then, though, she'd taken it. Loving him, yet hating him as well. Those days were long over.

Determined to have a showdown once and for all, she moved toward him. Alex raised an eyebrow at her, but stepped to the side, still gripping Stanley's upper arm. Everyone around her appeared to wait curiously, including her wealthy-but-rotten, low-life ex.

She poked him with a finger in the chest. A chest that was soft and pathetic in comparison to Chad's. Just one of hundreds of differences between the two men. "Your days of getting whatever you want are finished. You might have so-called friends and important connections back in Denver, but none here."

He snorted. "I'm important. You should remember that."

Whatever his problem was, it wasn't hers. She poked him again as he glared at her. "*Here* you are a worthless piece of shit." Realizing what she'd said, face heating, she glanced at her father, who stood listening attentively. "Sorry, Dad."

To her surprise, he looked proud as he said, "Fitting description, daughter."

Stanley focused on Chad, vowing, "I'm going to sue your ass off for assault." He concentrated on her again. "You too, bitch. I can't believe you had the nerve to kick me in the nuts."

Every man in the room flinched for a second in empathy. "First off, *you* hit Chad first. As for me, I should have done it years ago. Unfortunately, it wasn't until I escaped our marriage, and you, that I took karate lessons."

He growled and tried to lunge for her, gave an outraged growl that his hands were in cuffs behind him.

Alex jerked him away and shoved him none too gently toward the door. "It's time I got this asshole out of here." Her friend hesitated and looked sympathetically at her. "I hate to say this, but you and Chad are going to have to come to my office and sign the charges."

The fight and bluster had gone out of her; she began to tremble. Her stomach knotted. She'd gone to jail herself not long ago. She didn't look forward to going there again. Still, she managed to say quietly, "Yes, of course."

"Tomorrow," Chad interrupted and he stepped beside her. He draped his arm around her shoulders, gently squeezed them "That's soon enough."

"I will make you *all* pay for this," Stanley swore, glowering back at them.

Alex shook his head in disgust, not the least bit intimidated. He shoved the man out the front door. "Morning will be fine."

"If you need me to go with you, I will," her father said, gazing at her in worry. He'd been silent all this time, watching.

She was surprised by his offer, and yet not. He loved her no matter what mess she seemed to get into. She'd never forget the way her father and Alex had walked into the bedroom; both men looking stunned by the sight before them. Stanley being there was bad enough. Her in nothing but an afghan wrapped around her; Chad naked was worse. Humiliating. They had to have known what she and Chad had been doing prior to Stanley's arrival. Not the specifics, thank God. Still, what they suspected was enough. She would need hours of therapy to put this all behind her.

"I'll…I…" She couldn't look him in the eye. Then she gave a weak whimper, hating it, but unable to be strong any longer.

"Oh, honey." Her father took a step in her direction, stopping when Chad shook his head.

"I'll take care of her."

Chad's promise was reassuring. But her father appeared uncertain, then finally nodded.

After an awkward couple of seconds, Chad pulled her into his embrace. "I'll be there with her," he said. "If you feel you want to be present, that's up to you. But I can handle everything."

She buried her face against him, tears sliding down her cheeks, wetting his chest, but he didn't appear to care about that. He held her possessively, his strong arms comforting. Behind her, she heard her father leave and pull the door closed.

Chad held her for several minutes, but didn't say a word. She drew in steadying breaths, determined to stop being so weak. He was such a good man, easy to love. But she couldn't tell him how strong her feelings were. Although they'd grown closer - even intimate, he'd never said anything to make her believe he'd decided to take a chance on love again. He'd been shattered by his ex-wife's actions, lost his trust in women. If anyone could understand his pain, it was her. She wouldn't push him toward more than he was willing to give.

Stronger now, she eased back to look up at the handsome face etched with concern. "You don't have to stay." She swallowed down a sudden lump in her throat. "I know you have work things to do. I'll be okay. Really."

He shook his head, holding her gaze. "I'm not going anywhere. Whatever work I need to do can wait." And then he turned them both toward the bedroom. "I'm not okay. I need to -"

"I don't think I can go back to what we were doing," she said nervously. The humiliating images; him facing everyone naked, her naked and kneeling over the bed when Stanley had spotted her, were too much to get over this quickly.

"I wasn't implying sex, Antoinette. Although I'm never against the idea." He gave her a gentle look. "I just need to lie in bed beside you and hold you against me. I promise I won't do more than that."

***

Two days later, Toni sat numbly at her small desk, disheartened and apprehensive about her immediate future. Once again. Her life was a tangled web of complications. The issues with the house, and having to face that it would never be hers. Mending fences with her family. Wondering what she was going to do after her community service was up here in another twelve working days. The matter of Stanley and getting him permanently out of her life. And then there was Chad.

Even as exhausted as he'd had to be after leaving her apartment around midnight, he'd shown up on her doorstep right after sunrise. They'd gone together to the sheriff's office to sign the complaints against Stanley. Walking back in there had been hard because of her recent problem with the law. Neither Chad nor Alex had mentioned it and, fortunately, Stanley didn't know about it. She could only imagine his reaction, especially in his peculiar state of mind at the moment. Something had clearly driven him over the edge. She wondered about it, and yet couldn't make herself really care.

She fiddled with the pen beside her mouse by clicking it on and off, over and over. Monday had been awful. But yesterday had been almost as difficult. Chad had been so supportive, so good to her the entire time they were at the sheriff's office. He'd taken her home afterward and wanted to spend the day with her away from the office. She hadn't let him, although she'd taken the day off. Convincing him to leave and making him understand that she wanted to be alone to think took all of her limited acting ability. Agreeable but unhappy, he'd walked her to her door and then pulled her against him. He'd kissed her more passionately than she'd ever been kissed. When he'd released her to walk away, she'd seen his need to protect her written all over him. Yet he'd put that aside to give her what she needed.

She'd thought about that kiss the rest of the day, dreamt about it;

still almost felt the warm touch of his lips on hers. And she'd thought how seriously sexy he'd looked when he came to her place after work. His expressive eyes had been filled with longing and weariness. He hadn't shaved. She'd had to fight hard not to let him in, let him come to her bed. She'd sent him away.

The memory made her sigh with regret. Wanting him so intensely was testing her inner strength. It had been obvious how much he desired her, too. Yet he hadn't admitted to how he felt about her. His own life was as messy as hers. He had a staggering case load of elderly clients who needed his help. He was being pressured to move his practice solely to Topeka. And, even though they'd become lovers, he was cautious about protecting his heart. She had to protect hers as well.

The outer door opened and she heard familiar footsteps; not Chad's, his father's. Chad wouldn't be in today. When she'd arrived at the office, the temporary secretary had given her a message that he'd left.

In his quick, hard to decipher scrawl, he'd told her that he hadn't wanted to leave her until everything was settled about Stanley at his arraignment this morning. But something had come up in Topeka with Alberta Harper. He had to go, but he would call her later.

Her shoulders slumped with acceptance. One of these days he would make the decision to move to Topeka. How could he not? He already spent at least two days a week there, and could easily do more. Except that he was reluctant to leave the law practice with his father. And he'd become a bit obsessed about being with her.

But not enough to take their relationship a step further.

"Are you all right?" Ethan asked as he stepped into the doorway of the copy room.

Toni stilled her troubled thoughts and took a second before facing Chad's father. She wasn't sure how much he knew about her involvement with his son. At least he hadn't shown up at her apartment with her father and Alex. He hadn't found his son standing naked in her bedroom, her wearing only an afghan. And she continued to thank God that Stanley had been the only one to see her in such a humiliating, vulnerable position beside the bed, having obviously had sex with Chad. Although they'd been a long way from done when they'd been interrupted. Beside the point.

"Your father is worried about you," Ethan tried again to talk to her.

She sighed heavily. She'd put off seeing her family long enough, but she'd talked to her mother on the phone last night.

Finally she faced Ethan. "I'm going to have dinner with my family tonight." She'd agreed reluctantly to the commitment. But it would be hard to look her father in the eyes after what he'd witnessed.

Ethan gave her a look of approval. Then his expression darkened. "Your ex-husband is going to be arraigned later this morning."

"He'll get off with hardly more than a slap on his hands. His family will see to it." Bitterness spread through her. But all she wanted was him out of her town, out of her life forever. Between the restraining order and the Beatons she hoped it would happen.

Ethan's mouth thinned and he said, "I hate to say it, but that's probably true. They're powerful, with lots of influence all over the Midwest."

"It really doesn't matter anymore. I only want him gone."

He nodded in understanding and changed the subject. "I'm so sorry about the legal problems with this house, for all of us. Chad told me the whole situation." He watched her carefully. "I got a call from William Carter yesterday. Their attorney has received the final signature needed to be able to have a clear title."

Chad hadn't mentioned it to her, but then he'd probably gotten tied up with handling the situation with Mrs. Harper. She forced a smile. "Then you and Chad will soon have the legal ability to buy the house. It's only right, considering all the money you've invested here."

"Yes, we have. Again, I'm sorry about your part of the Caruthers brothers' fraud scheme. They're been searched for, but…"

"I've already accepted that my considerable payment to them is long gone. I can live with the expensive lesson in being more careful in further business dealings." The loss of twenty thousand dollars was considerable, but considering how little it was in comparison to her larger than expected divorce settlement, it wasn't that much.

He glanced at the clock on the wall, frowning. "I'm going to the courthouse to represent you and Chad at Beaton's arraignment. If necessary. With Alex's testimony, I doubt I will be needed." After a second, he asked, "Do you want to go with me?"

She shook her head. "I'd prefer to never see my ex-husband again." Nor did she want to face her memories of being in the courtroom to face her own charges.

"I understand. My son and I will do our best to see that you never have to." He gave her a final sympathetic look and left.

Stanley was her problem, not theirs. Besides, Chad wouldn't be around to watch after her when he moved away. And she was sure he would. The idea sickened her. But she needed to move past her disappointment, past the loss of this house, past the short amount of time she had left working here. She'd stay in the apartment for now, but she would start looking for another place to live and another job to keep her busy. She never wanted to be one of the idle rich, even if she could afford to be that.

Sadness filled her as she glanced around her cramped temporary office. She would miss being here, miss Ethan and especially Chad.

Chapter Eleven

Exhaustion washed over Chad as he sat next to his father in the courtroom, waiting for Stanley's appearance before the judge. Somehow, the arraignment had been postponed an extra day. He was thankful for that because he'd wanted to be here. But he'd had to work all day the day before and long into the night so he could hurry back.

He yawned and pulled in a deep breath. His eyes felt gritty from lack of sleep. He hadn't gotten home until four o'clock, and sleep had evaded him. His mind wouldn't shut down. He was juggling too many balls in the air; so many people needed his help. And there was the group in Topeka who were still pressuring him. His head throbbed with a pounding headache. The only thing good at the moment was that he'd see Toni again sometime today.

"You okay, son?" his father asked, lightly patting Chad's leg to get his attention. "You should have stayed home to rest. I'm here to represent you and Toni, if necessary. But I think Alex has this covered. And I filed the restraining order yesterday."

"I wouldn't have been able to sleep for worrying about the SOB getting off far too easily." He hesitated and looked around the courtroom. An older couple in fine clothes, and appearing bored and a bit annoyed to be here, sat on the far side of the gallery. "I'm pretty sure that's why the Beatons are here."

Ethan glimpsed in their direction and frowned. "You're probably right. I don't think Judge Turner will be impressed. He hates politics and people who try to show off their power. He's also developed sort of a sweet spot for Toni, having been watching her behavior since coming before him last month. The man doesn't miss anything."

The judge fined the defendant in front of his bench and dismissed him. When he looked up, he noticed first the Beatons and then Chad and his father. He had a serious poker face. It was always hard to tell exactly how he leaned on a matter until he gave his decision. Yet from what his father had said, Chad had a feeling the judge was disgusted with what he'd heard about some of Toni's marital problems. He was well connected to the community's gossip vine.

The doors opened and Stanley Beaton strode inside, dressed in a tailored suit his parents must have brought for him to wear. His hair was neatly combed; his face freshly shaved. Confidence reeked from him as he moved by Chad, barely glancing at him.

He stopped at the gate leading from the gallery to the counsel tables. He stiffened his shoulders and said coolly, "Judge, this whole matter is a waste of the court's time and money." He glowered at Alex, who had moved next to him. "I'm going to press charges against the sheriff for wrongful arrest, speak to the Kansas Bar Association about…"

Judge Turner pounded his gavel on the bench. "I believe it is time for you to shut the hell up, Beaton."

Beaton puffed up in outrage.

Beaton senior shot to his feet and protested, "My son is right, your Honor. This whole situation is such a farce. And keeping him in jail for almost 72 hours is beyond irresponsible."

To everyone's surprise, the judge stood, hands flattened on the bench in front of him. He leaned forward and glowered first at Stanley and then his father. "Your son is dead wrong and so are you. I don't care what you're worth. I don't care what ridiculous influence you think you have. None of that matters in *my* courtroom. Now sit the hell down or I will have you removed from here."

Face red in fury, Beaton sat down, muttering to his wife about small towns and small town judges. Except his voice carried throughout the room.

The judge took his seat again, ignored the grumbling older Beaton, and focused on Stanley. "From what I have heard, young man, you are a piece of work. You abused your ex-wife. You used your supposed wealth and influence to make sure it was *she* who came off as the bad guy. But you mean absolutely nothing in Petersville. Other than a man who should have gone to jail a long time ago."

Stanley's hands fisted at his sides. He gritted out, "Whatever you think you know are lies that my whoring ex-wife has spread."

Chad got his feet, but remained quiet when the judge looked at him and shook his head. With great reluctance, he sat back down.

"Let the judge handle this, son. He knows what he's doing," Ethan said quietly.

"I'm not going to get a fair hearing here. You're biased already," Stanley bit out.

Judge Turner heaved a sigh of disgust that everyone in the courtroom heard. "This *is not* a hearing, Mr. Beaton. This is an arraignment on several misdemeanor charges that have been brought against you."

Stanley stiffened again, hands clenching at his sides again. "But these charges will be on my record, until I seek a misdemeanor expungement."

The double doors opened once more, interrupting the tense situation. Chad gaped at Toni standing there. He'd hoped she would stay away from this. But she didn't even look in his direction. Instead she glared in irritation at Beaton.

"What the hell are you doing here?" Beaton snarled. "This whole problem is your fault. I'm going to…"

Senior Beaton was on his feet again, this time focusing on his son. "You are only making matters worse. Be a man, for God's sake, and face the consequences of your actions." Then he turned to his wife. "Come on. We're leaving. It's time we stopped coddling him. Time he took responsibility."

Stanley stood rigidly as his parents left the courtroom. A second later he seemed to deflate, like a balloon losing its air.

"Maybe now we can actually get down to business," the judge said, getting everyone's attention once more.

Stanley didn't turn around, though. He looked straight at Toni, his brow furrowing, but he didn't say a word.

Toni slipped onto the pew next to Ethan, who gave her a gentle smile.

Walking back into this courtroom had been almost as hard as the first time. Her stomach was knotted with nerves. She shivered inside her coat, pulling it closer. She glanced at Chad and his father, whispering, "I had to come. I had to…" She stopped talking. She just had to be here. Period.

Ethan reached over to squeeze her hand in support.

"I've been told that you chose not to have a lawyer for this arraignment, Mr. Beaton," the judge captured everyone's attention. "Which is for the best."

Stanley straightened his back and faced the judge. "I didn't find it necessary." He didn't sound quite as arrogant as she'd overheard him from outside the door.

His parents had walked right past her, hesitating, and then hurrying away. They'd come to be there for their son, but something had changed their minds about staying. Stanley was on his own to defend his actions; no doubt for the first time in his life. Maybe she should feel sorry for him, but she didn't.

"The defendant, Stanley Beaton, will now approach the bench," the judge said formally. He watched as Stanley took another few seconds before doing as requested.

"Mr. Beaton, you are charged with multiple misdemeanors. You are charged with disorderly conduct, trespassing in your ex-wife's apartment without permission, engaging in violent behavior, and assault to Chadwin Anderson."

Toni shifted uneasily in her seat. She'd faced some of the same charges, which she still regretted. But she didn't feel like the same person who had returned to her hometown a month ago. She was no longer insecure, even though she needed to find a new place to live and a job. She no longer cowered when someone around her raised their voice. Her future held a lot of uncertainties, but she now felt she could handle them. Thanks to Ethan and Chad and her father. Mostly thanks to Chad.

She glanced at him, finding him studying her with a worried expression. Then she noticed the elastic bandage was gone from his arm and smiled in relief.

Judge Turner cleared his throat before continuing. "Do you understand the charges, Mr. Beaton?"

Stanley huffed, then grumbled, "Yes."

"Good. Now what is your plea, Mr. Beaton? Not guilty. No contest. Guilty?" He looked intently at him. "I assume you know the differences."

"I still believe…"

"Mr. Beaton, each and every one of the charges is correct. There were witnesses; evidence to the assault on Mr. Anderson's person."

Stanley looked back at Toni and she sucked in a breath, but forced herself not to flinch. Anger filled his expression. He faced the judge again. "What about *her*? She assaulted me."

Did the corner of the judge's mouth just twitch? Toni waited nervously.

"Sheriff Crampton tells me it was done in defense of Mr. Anderson." The judge studied Stanley pointedly. "You understand that Reverend Thomas Thornton was also a witness."

"He's her father. Of course he would back her up." He appeared to deflate again as he obviously remembered his own father didn't have his back any longer. Still he explained, "She kicked me in the balls, your Honor."

Toni sensed every man in the courtroom flinching in empathy. But Judge Turner simply said, "Good for her, bad for you. But that is beside the point here, Mr. Beaton. Again I ask, what is your plea?"

It took Stanley several awkward seconds before he stated, "Guilty, your Honor."

Toni breathed a sigh of relief and Chad reached over to squeeze her thigh. "It appears your ex has some backbone after all," he said in a lowered voice.

"Because he's dealing with this alone," she countered, but couldn't help feeling better.

Chad sat back and she noted how Ethan gave a slight grin. Was he thinking the two of them would eventually become a real couple? That they'd get married? Her heart pinched. He'd be wrong. Maybe they would continue some kind of relationship; bed buddies, and lovers. That's all it could be, even if she might want more. She had to fully accept that Chad would be moving away. His work life wasn't here any longer.

"You will pay a fine of $500 on each of the charges, for a total of $2000," Judge Turner said in a blunt manner.

Toni blinked back to the moment. It was a pittance, considering the millions Stanley was worth. But it was something. The charges hadn't just been dismissed.

"Fine," Stanley agreed in annoyance.

"That's not all, Mr. Beaton." The judge looked sternly at him. "I could also sentence you to thirty days in jail. Instead I'm going to be lenient, although I doubt you deserve it. You are additionally sentenced to thirty days of community service."

Here? Oh, God. Toni held still, worrying.

"You have got to be kidding me," Stanley complained. "I don't have time for such nonsense. I'm a busy man."

"Well, you're going to be busier. Unless you prefer to sit in jail for that same length of time?"

Stanley kept his mouth shut, which was a definite surprise.

"I will arrange to see to it that you can serve your community service in Denver. We'd all prefer you to leave town and not return."

The judge looked at Toni and Chad as well. "I'm sure you are aware that a restraining order has been filed. You are not to come anywhere near Ms. Thornton."

"But I…"

"No buts about it, Mr. Beaton. You need to accept that your divorce is final; that she isn't your wife, and that she's not interested in being so ever again." It was clear that the judge had been told about Stanley's insistence that he wanted to take her back with him; ignore the divorce.

Toni watched Stanley steel his spine, sensed his anger. She still didn't know *why* he wanted her back. And she didn't care. It was *his* problem, not hers.

"Do we understand each other, Mr. Beaton? You will have nothing more to do with your ex-wife. And you will be leaving town today." "Yes, your Honor," Stanley grumbled. "I've decided I am no longer interested in trying to make things work with her."

Toni felt free of him, really free of him for the first time. She slumped in relief, smiling.

"Good decision. Now, Alex, escort him out of my courtroom. Then make sure he leaves town as soon as he's gathered up whatever he brought with him."

She was still leaning back, taking it all in, when Alex walked toward them with Stanley.

Stanley stopped next to her and frowned down in what almost appeared to be hatred. "I don't know what I was thinking, wanting you back. Clearly I'd been drinking too much. You never were a good wife to me." He focused on Chad. "She's not even good in bed."

Chad stood immediately and started to move toward Stanley, but Ethan grabbed his arm to stop him.

Toni felt humiliated, especially with Ethan and Alex listening, probably the judge as well. Both the men around her appeared disgusted, not with her, but with Stanley. Her loser of an ex-husband.

In the next instant, she shot to her feet. She got right in Stanley's face and was pleased when he actually took a step backward. He covered his privates. At last she had power over him, even if she didn't want it. "You were the world's worst husband. Everything was about *you.* I was just there to do whatever you wished." She took a second and asked, "Why exactly did you come here?"

"It was a huge mistake that I'll never make again. Believe me, you are not worth all you cost me in the divorce settlement." He glowered back at Alex and the judge still at the bench. "Or the trouble you've caused me here."

She eased back and glanced down where he continued to protect himself. She ignored his last comment and went back to the sex issue. "I might have been better in bed, if you'd been a decent man." She met his wary eyes. "Or if you had more than a puny penis."

Stanley snarled and moved toward her, but Alex grabbed his arm and pulled him away. "Let's go. Now. You're already going against the restraining order."

Her ex-husband gritted his teeth, gave her a dismissive look, and stormed out of the courtroom. "Whore!"

Ethan chuckled behind her. But when she turned, she found Chad studying her, and he didn't appear happy. He didn't speak; certainly didn't seem as amused as his father had been. Her stomach sank. She'd been too crude. He hadn't expected her to defend herself. Well, the hell with him!

She spun away to speed out of the courtroom. Her first thought as she stepped into the hallway was that she really needed a drink.

Then she froze, horrified.

No! She didn't. It was just being around Stanley. Drinking and letting her mind go numb had been easier for her to deal with him. She wasn't an alcoholic. But alcohol had been her crutch and it never would be again. She all but ran, needing to get out of the building, needing to breathe fresh air.

"Toni, wait!" Chad called after her.

She didn't even turn back toward him. He'd let her down, or maybe she'd come to expect too much from him. That wasn't fair. He'd been good to her, especially considering that she'd basically attacked him in a fit of temper. Still, she needed to get away for now.

***

Chad sat in his office, but he couldn't focus on anything. Except Toni. He'd come back here with his father after leaving the courthouse. His father had warned him to leave her alone and not go after her. She needed to process all that had happened. He'd also told Chad that he'd let her down after she'd defended herself to Beaton and not said a word of support. He'd hurt her with his silence.

He glanced at his monitor, at the client's file that he was supposed to be working on today. The words were a blur, so he leaned back in his chair and closed his eyes. He had to make sense of everything. She hadn't been the only one upset by Beaton. He'd been livid when the bastard had called her a whore. His father had been right to stop him, or he would have laid into the man, probably been taken to jail for assault. Exactly what none of them needed. Still, the vile name rolled over and over in his mind. He longed to slam his fist into Beaton's face.

Then he replayed her verbal attack on her ex-husband, *puny penis*. While Beaton had puffed up in fury, Chad's father had chuckled. He hadn't. He'd been stunned by what she'd said, caught off guard. He'd felt proud of her for finally defending herself against the man who'd made her life hell. Yet he'd just stood there, shocked, and uncertain what to say or do. Which was why she'd run from him. She hadn't even hesitated to give him a chance to explain.

And she hadn't come back to the office to finish the workday. Her car wasn't even in the parking lot, so she wasn't in her apartment, either. She'd gone somewhere. But where? He'd called her parents, her brother, even Ellen, who had become her friend. Nobody knew where she was. He couldn't help worrying. He wanted to go looking for her, but his father continued to tell him to give her time and space. She'd been through a lot for a long time, including today. When she was ready, she'd be back. But he had an uneasy feeling about that. He worried that whatever had started between them might have taken a serious setback.

He opened his eyes and heaved a frustrated breath. He'd failed her, but he hadn't meant to. Lord, he would never hurt her. She was precious to him. Truthfully, he was pretty sure that he loved her. He couldn't tell her, though. No woman wanted to have a man tell her he was "pretty sure" that he was in love with her. He might actually love her, but their past and his past complicated everything. She'd gone off with another man just when he was finally ready to start something with her. That had disappointed and angered him for years. He'd eventually decided to give marriage a chance with someone else, which had been a huge mistake. When Sandy had admitted to an abortion, it had crushed him. He couldn't count on women; didn't trust them.

Yet he knew that wasn't true with Toni. They'd both gone through a lot in their failed marriages. He'd wanted to help her heal and put that horror behind her. In the process, she'd helped him as well. They'd become friends. More than that. They'd become lovers. Still, the relationship was so new, so fragile. He didn't think she was ready to become really involved with another man. Besides, his life was a disaster at the moment. And even though he'd gotten over some of the bitterness from Sandy's betrayal, he still guarded his heart. Toni deserved better than a man who couldn't fully move on from his past.

His father was probably right about him giving her time to adjust to what had happened today. He figured she was mad at him at the moment for good reason. It was best to give her space right now. Hopefully, when she showed up again at either her apartment or the office, they could talk this issue out. Maybe he wasn't ready to completely commit to a life-long relationship, including marriage, but he didn't want to lose her. Not again. He just needed more time to work through his issues and let go of his pain.

"Mr. Anderson," Debi, their temporary secretary, said from his doorway. "I forgot to give you your messages when you got here an hour ago. Some of the people have called repeatedly." The mid-thirties woman, already graying, walked to his desk and handed him the imposing stack of pink phone messages. Her thin lips pursed in annoyance. "What am I supposed to do about all the copies Ms. Thornton was supposed to make today?"

He wasn't up to her pissy attitude. To his disgust, she had never warmed to Toni, like Ellen had. If she hadn't been a good receptionist, and more than capable as a legal secretary, he would have already let her go. "She needed the day off," he said flatly. He didn't want to talk about the matter more than that.

But she didn't take the hint. She huffed and shook her head. "Will the court allow that? I believe she still owes you another twelve days."

Twelve days? The thirty days was going by far too fast. He didn't want her to leave the office; wanted her to stay on, but she'd told him no. He understood her reasoning, but he still hoped he could change her mind. He liked her being at the office, even on the days he wasn't.

He put his frustration with that situation aside and looked pointedly at Mrs. Hamilton. "It isn't your concern. I'm confident that Ms. Thornton will give us the full time ordered by the court."

Again, he tried to end the discussion. He shifted his concentration to the stack of messages that he wasn't in the mood to return. Especially to Heath Oxford, who was getting on Chad's nerves about pressing him to make a decision concerning moving his practice to Topeka. It might be best for a number of reasons and for his position as a strong leader in the group of elder abuse lawyers. He had the most experience. Yet he couldn't seem to make that decision, either way.

To his annoyance, the secretary hadn't moved. He sensed her resentment, then heard it in her voice. "I believe you are far too lenient with her, because you..." She stopped talking, but it was too late in his opinion.

He narrowed his eyes. "Because I have feelings for Ms. Thornton? Because you disapprove of her, when you don't really know her?"

Her pointed chin went up. "I know enough." She didn't respond to his admission of feelings for Toni.

He'd had enough. "I believe we can do without your services any longer, Mrs. Hamilton. You can leave immediately after you gather your personal things."

She blinked in astonishment. "You're *firing* me? Because I'm not Ms. Thornton's BFF? I shouldn't have to be her friend, or even supportive of her. You pay me to work, which I do."

"I never expected you to become buddy-buddy with Ms. Thornton. I - we, Dad and I - did expect you to get along with her. I've seen absolutely no signs of that. Neither has my father." He nodded toward the door. "We'll pay you for your two weeks' notice. Because you are a competent legal secretary, I won't fire you for overstepping your boundaries here. I'm letting you go."

She glared at him in disbelief for a few seconds. When he didn't back down from his decision, she strode out of his office.

His Dad was going to love this new problem, wonder at his son's sanity. Well, too damn bad. There were enough complications in his life. He wasn't going to keep putting up with a secretary with a bad attitude.

***

The rock she'd tossed into the pond in the small park just outside of town rippled the water briefly before sinking. Toni had come here many times growing up; playing on the various playground equipment, picnicking with her family, trailing after her brother and Chad as they'd found their favorite fishing spot and tried to discourage her from following them. There were a lot of memories here, good ones. Her memories of the last six years weren't anywhere close to being good. But she was ready to make a new life and make some new memories that she could look back on and not hurt.

She attempted to make another rock skip across the water, but it sunk immediately. She'd never been good at it. Of all the people in her life back then, Chad had been the one to patiently work with her on developing the skill. Ted had only teased her about her incompetence at rock skipping. Even with Chad being five years older than her, there were other instances she remembered when he had done things with her. It had been a long time since she'd thought about them.

Staring out at the water, pulling her coat tighter around her, Toni allowed the warm memories to resurface. She'd been sixteen when Chad had come home from college for the town's annual parade and dance. Standing at the back of the big community hall, she'd watched him walk in with her brother, both of them with dates hanging on their arms. Envy had curled through her. Her date for the event had changed his mind. Brooding, she'd kept to herself. But Chad had spotted her at the moment she was blinking back tears. She'd tried to move further away from everyone. A few minutes later he found her. He'd stopped in front of her, smiled gently, and then led her onto the dancefloor. She hadn't resisted. It had only been for the one dance, but it was one of her most special memories.

Chad. Her heart pinched just thinking about him.

She knew taking off on a spur of the moment decision wasn't a mature reaction to his hesitation to support her after she'd confronted Stanley. She didn't hold it against him, not really. That wasn't the real issue, not why she'd hurried away.

Shivering from the cool wind, she watched a pair of ducks land on the pond. Somehow the way they simply swam together comforted her. If only her life were that simple.

She'd been overwhelmed by everything that had gone on in the courtroom. Facing her former in-laws had been unexpected. Their not acknowledging her presence was not a surprise. More importantly, Stanley had gotten to her again, for a few minutes. The pretentious fool still believed he was in charge of everything; that he could get away with anything.

She smiled remembering how Judge Turner hadn't been impressed by her ex-husband's attitude or his family's influence. Even though he'd given her a thirty-day sentence for community service, she'd accepted his decision with no objection. The responsibility for what she'd done lay only with her. And, in truth, she'd come to like being at the law firm. Ethan was a good man, always having a kind word for her. Ellen had become a new friend. Chad…Well, that was where it got complicated.

In another two weeks she would be done working for the firm. An emptiness filled her. But she was right in that they didn't need her. She intended to stop in the Dine-In Café later today and talk to Elsie Mae and Harold, the owners. Years ago, she had worked there one summer. She hadn't been too bad at waitressing, so, hopefully, they would give her another chance. She didn't need it to be a long-term job. All she was looking for now was something to fill her time until she found another house in town or around it that needed some TLC. She wasn't scared of hard work and she would enjoy giving some tender loving care to a house that she could make into something she could live in for a long time.

Her cell phone rang and she pulled it out of her coat pocket. She glanced at the caller ID, Ellen?

"Are you all right? Is something wrong with the baby?" Toni asked in concern. She still hadn't gone to see them. Somehow time had slipped away, but they'd talked on the phone.

"No. It's nothing like that," Ellen reassured her, sounding happy. "I know of the perfect house for you. Actually, my husband's great aunt Gracie Yardley owns it."

Toni listened eagerly. She would be certain to fully check this out, though. She'd learned her lesson the hard way about not being careful. "This won't be another problem for me?" she asked, trying not to sound rude. But Ellen knew about what had happened with the Victorian house the law firm had attempted to buy at the same time she had. And Ellen knew the law firm would end up being the new owners.

"I understand your wariness, but this won't be a problem. I promise you that."

Relief lessened her tension; hope filled her. "Tell me about it."

"It's a big, old farmhouse with touches of Victorian details. The farm itself was sold off long ago when her husband died. But Gracie kept the house, except she hasn't maintained it very well. Actually, it needs a lot of fixing up."

"Where is it at? Can I see it?"

Ellen laughed at her eagerness. "The family moved Gracie out a month ago, to a nursing home. She needs the money from selling the house. But we all know it isn't worth much, because of all that needs to be done to it." She hesitated. "But, Toni, I've seen it and I think it is everything you want. A challenge for now, but I'm sure it will be a beautiful home when you get done with it."

That sounded like exactly what she wanted: a challenge and a home of her own. She listened as Ellen gave her directions so she could go see it, at least on the outside for now. Her spirits were lifted when she disconnected the call. Maybe things were finally looking up for her.

As she walked back to her car, she thought about Chad. Their situation was still a problem. He would be leaving and she would miss him. But she wouldn't try to stop him. She could stand on her own now, partly because of him helping her find her self-confidence again. Partly because she'd moved on from what Stanley had done to her. She was finding herself all over again. And that felt good.

Chapter Twelve

Chad sat in the chair opposite Alex's desk, waiting while his friend took an important call. He'd been out of town for the last eight long days and was ready to deal with issues here. He'd wanted to go to breakfast with his Dad and discuss the Topeka problem. And he wanted to get to the office and see Toni. His time away had happened unexpectedly because some meetings and court hearings had been rescheduled for sooner than he'd planned. He hadn't even had a chance to say goodbye to her, because he hadn't been able to find her before he'd had to get on the road. They'd talked a few times by phone, but their conversations had been strained. It worried him.

He glanced at his watch and frowned. While he understood Alex's need to tend to business, he, too, had matters to handle. If his friend hadn't caught him on the way out the door to meet his Dad, he would already be...

Interrupting his thoughts, Alex waved at him from across the large room. "Let's talk in here."

Evidently they needed privacy, which made Chad curious. He got up to follow the other man into the small interrogation room. As he took a seat by the table, Alex closed the door.

"So, what's up?" he asked, wondering why Alex had insisted on this early meeting. "Something going on with Beaton? Is he trying to cause problems?" They'd talked about Beaton a number of times while Chad had been gone. He'd been reassured that Toni's ex-husband had left Petersville, and that he'd gotten assigned community service in Denver. But he wouldn't be surprised if the man somehow found a way to make trouble again.

Alex pulled the other chair around and straddled it. "I think we're done with that man. What an asshole!" He shook his head. "I have no idea what Toni ever saw in him, but then she was younger and ready to fall in love. Too bad it was with the wrong man."

Chad nodded agreement. He'd been younger back then, too, and stupid. He'd missed his opportunity with her, regretting it for a long time. But he was getting a second chance. He wouldn't screw it up this time...unless she wasn't willing to wait for him to get his head straight.

"She's a fine looking woman now, grown up and single again." Alex looked at him, his eyes solemn as he pulled Chad from his troubled thoughts.

"I can't argue with any of that." Something was going here and it made him uneasy. "Again, what is this about? I have a feeling it's not just for idle chit-chat." He studied his friend, concerned. "Does this have anything to do with what has been bothering you lately?"

"No, it isn't to chit-chat, as you put it." Alex's brow furrowed, and then he pressed, "What are your intentions toward Toni?"

His intentions? "Seriously?"

"Seriously."

Chad was uncomfortable with the topic. He didn't know exactly what his "intentions" were, other than getting to know each other better. And hoping for more, if they could talk their latest hiccup out. "You're not her father. What does it matter to you?"

Alex blew out a deep breath and still looked intense. "Because she's a good friend. Because she's vulnerable now, emotionally. I don't want to see her hurt again."

"A good friend?" Sure, Alex had been around her most of her life, almost as much as he had. But they'd never been much more than acquaintances. Or so he'd thought. Had something been going on between them while he'd been away? He narrowed his eyes. "Am I missing something here?"

It took Alex a couple of seconds before he answered. "She needed some advice while you've been gone. About a house she's buying. Advice about construction and remodeling issues."

And Alex's father had owned a construction company until he'd died five years ago. Alex had worked with the company in high school. He'd inherited the company when he'd left the service and mainly managed it now, while a reliable crew did the work. But he had a great deal of knowledge on the subject.

"She mentioned that she was looking at an older house." She hadn't told him that she was actually in the buying process. Separated just over a week and already they were growing apart. It worried him.

"It's gone way past looking. She should be signing the final papers next week." Alex met Chad's gaze, held it. "Back to your intentions, buddy. It's obvious you've been intimate with her at least once, maybe more."

Chad stiffened; uncomfortable talking about his relationship with Toni. "That really is a personal matter." He'd hated that his friend had found him naked and her in only an afghan in her bedroom. Her father had as well. He'd tried not to think about that awkward situation, although he couldn't forget it.

"Like I said, she's susceptible at the moment to…"

Leaning forward in his chair, Chad frowned and his friend stopped talking. "You don't think I know that? I've seen her crying. I've seen her broken. It kills me."

"Yet you've been gone…"

"Because I had to be there for those hearings, for those damn meetings. You know that." Hadn't he been frustrated enough with the problem? Hadn't he worried about Toni and how she seemed to be pulling back from him? Hell, yes!

Alex nodded, then thrust his chin out. "Okay, it was necessary. But, dammit, Chad, she's important to me, too."

"As an old friend?"

Alex avoided meeting Chad's eyes. "She was too young for me back then. We weren't even really friends. But now…"

"Back then?" Chad's frown deepened, his stomach knotted. "Are you telling me that you're romantically interested in Toni? That you'd pursue her if I weren't involved with her?" The idea was like a punch to the gut. Alex was a good-looking man, but he'd always gone from one woman to the next. None of his break-ups had been bad. He hadn't been ready to settle down. Was he now? With Toni? *God, no.*

"That's precisely what I'm telling you. She needs a man who will take care of her, share his life with her…be around." Alex pinned Chad with a challenging look. "Maybe you've been watching over her." His jaw tightened. "Been intimate with her. But you're not looking for more than a temporary bed partner. Sandy did a real job on you; made you resistant to the idea of marrying again."

"She damn sure did." Why couldn't he let that go? Still, he didn't like to cheapen what he had with Toni at the moment. They'd only made love together that one time, but it had been amazing. Their next effort had turned into a complicated, humiliating disaster.

He focused on his friend. "You don't care that she and I have been together in her bed? You want to go after her, if I'm out of the picture?"

Alex nodded. "That's why I asked you to come here this morning. You're one of my closest friends. I need to know if..."

"She's mine," Chad protested. But was she really? Or were they merely both reacting on the rebound, although he'd dated many times since divorcing Sandy. He didn't actually believe that. At least he didn't want to think that way. She'd become very special to him.

"Yet you're not willing to take the next step. In fact, you're moving away. So where does that leave Toni?" Alex gave him a hard look. "I'm ready to find the right woman and take the step that scares the hell out of you."

Chad tried to control his temper, but he'd reached the peak of his frustration level. "And you think your 'right woman' would be Toni?"

"I think she could be. I'd like to ask her out, see if she might be interested in someone besides you."

"Hell, man, you're killing me. Pressuring me, like those lawyers in Topeka." He stood and tried to calm down. He didn't want to fight with his old friend. He also didn't like the idea of Alex wanting to get to know Toni better. He pushed the subject aside for now. "How did you hear that I was moving away? Even *I* don't know that for sure."

Alex stood as well, but he leaned a hip on the table to focus on Chad. "Your Dad told me, and he's pretty sure you will. It's a good business decision, according to him. But he's worried about the situation, too."

"What situation?" He should have known his father would have already heard about Chad's problem in Topeka. His Dad had connections with attorneys all over the state.

"You and Toni. He likes her a lot and, like me, doesn't want to see her get hurt any more than she has been." He frowned again and they locked gazes. "We both - your Dad and I - know that's going to happen. I think she cares for you. A lot. But she won't say anything because she doesn't want to influence you either way." He blew out a breath. "That's my opinion, though."

Alex's opinion about her not trying to stop him about the Topeka matter was right on the money. Actually, she'd even encouraged him because she knew it would be good for his career. It seemed everyone had accepted that leaving was the choice he'd make. He was the only one not convinced yet.

Chad strode toward the door, gripped the handle, and faced Alex once more. "My decision hasn't been made yet. Regardless of that, I wish you'd all stay out of our personal business. Meaning, back off."

"I will…until you walk away from the best thing that could ever happen to you. Then I'm going after her."

Chad jerked the door open and strode out. He caught the way Alex's secretary, Bella, gave him a disapproving look, but he kept on walking. It wasn't until he stepped onto the sidewalk that his shoulders lost the tight tension that had begun when Alex admitted he might be interested in Toni. Damn, as if his life wasn't difficult enough. Now his friend was ready to step in if he was out of the way. He hated that. He couldn't deny that she was a beautiful, tempting woman. With the right man, she could be happy the rest of her life. She would be more careful in picking that man this time.

He went to his car and climbed inside. Could he be the man she would want to take a chance on? Alex had said she cared for him. He already knew she trusted him, because she wouldn't have taken him to her bed otherwise that first time. But did she really have strong feelings for him? His heart tightened with hope. Yet he knew they still had problems to work out.

Taking a drive might help him think things over. He wasn't ready to talk to his father yet, understanding his worry about him hurting her. He wasn't ready to find Toni at the moment either. He decided to head back to Topeka, planning to weigh everything over in his mind. The move there would be good for his career, but was it necessary? He'd been doing all right before this issue came up. He handled his workload here and still spent time in Topeka when needed. Besides, he had clients here that he was still helping, like Alberta Harper. Which reminded him that he should check on her while he was in Topeka.

He started the car, but took another second to mull over his difficult conversation with Alex. Was he willing to back off from what he'd started with Toni? No. Could he live with seeing her with another man? With Alex? God, he seriously loathed that idea. But was he thinking only of himself and not about what would be best for her?

***

"Of course, honey, we'll hire you," Elsie Mae said as she sat with Toni in one of the booths that evening after the rush of diners left. "I thought you were happy working at the law firm."

"I was, but it's time for me to move on," she said quietly. "My community service duties will be done next Friday." Her face heated in embarrassment at the painful subject. She had to swallow hard at thinking about actually leaving the firm. With that snooty Debi Hamilton gone, things had gone better this week. She and Ethan had gotten along really well, and she'd been able to keep up with what he'd needed. But Ellen would be coming back in a couple of weeks, earlier than originally planned.

Elsie Mae nodded and looked sympathetic. "If you'd like to, you can start here next week. If you change your mind and want to go back to Anderson and Anderson, we'll understand."

"I'm really not qualified to be a secretary. I can answer the phone, yes, but otherwise I don't belong there. They don't need me, especially with Ellen coming back sooner than expected." She studied her hands, glanced at the white spot on her ring finger. She wondered how long it would take for the whiteness to fade away.

She sensed the other woman watching her and looked up again. "I only need a part-time job, and maybe just for a short time."

"I heard you got a good divorce settlement from that louse of an ex-husband. Why work at all?" Elsie Mae asked curiously.

The Petersville gossip vine had been active. Toni wasn't sure how anyone had found out about the settlement, but it didn't matter. "I need to keep busy. Until I can actually move into Gracie Yardley's house, which I'm sure you've heard that I'm buying."

"She really let the place go. It'll take some serious work."

Toni definitely knew that, but the inspectors she'd hired to look the house over thought it was basically sound. And Alex had helped her talk through all that needed to be repaired or replaced. She'd thought he'd sold his father's construction business. Learning that he hadn't and that he'd enjoy the challenge of working on her house had lightened her spirits. Plus he'd turned into a good friend. He was easy to talk to, although he didn't generally say much, just let her babble on. Still, she liked him a lot. Not in the same way she did Chad, sadly.

"Working on the house will be good, for a lot of reasons. I don't want to have too much time to think about missing…" She stopped; shocked that she'd let that slip out.

Elsie Mae gently patted Toni's had where it lie on the tabletop. "We've all heard about Chad moving away. I'm so sorry. I know you two have been seeing each other."

To her mortification, tears filled Toni's eyes. Everything with Chad was so complicated. He'd been gone since the evening of Stanley's arraignment. Ethan said he'd gotten a call that the important court hearings on some new elder abuse laws had been moved up and he'd had to leave. He'd explained that when he'd called her. She understood, of course. But she'd been hurt anyway that he hadn't seen her before leaving town. Her own fault, though. She'd made herself scarce that day.

"It will be good for his career. Certainly safer than having him drive back and forth to Topeka so often." She really worried about him on those trips, even if they weren't long drives.

"I suppose that's true."

She pulled her hand away from the kind woman's hold and got up. Blinking back the tears that she refused to shed, she asked in a shaking voice, "I'll see you on Monday for the breakfast and lunch shifts, right?"

"Don't give up on him," Elsie Mae protested. "Maybe he'll come to his senses and ask you to..."

Toni shook her head and her heart hurt. "He's told me that he won't ever get married again. He didn't say as much, but I know he's afraid to risk his heart." Not even for her. But she hadn't told him about her feelings for him, which might have changed his mind. She couldn't, though. She had to let him move on with his life and she would move on with rebuilding hers.

Elsie looked ready to protest once more, but Toni didn't want to hear it. She was done fretting over Chad and what could have been. Maybe she'd accept the date with Alex after all. He'd stopped by her apartment last night to ask her out. She'd refused, but now she'd reconsider the idea, even if it didn't feel right.

She hurried out of the café in the middle of Main Street and hardly noticed where she was walking. She just had to get to her car. With each step she took, she knew she'd have to make sure Alex understood that she could only be his friend. She wasn't ready to go out with someone else. She might never be ready. It was too painful to fall in love and then...

"Can we talk?"

Her heart raced at the sound of Chad's deep voice. She looked up and found him leaning against her car parked beneath a lamppost. His eyes mirrored exhaustion, concern. But could she survive talking to him now when she was already trying to get used to the idea of him being gone? She didn't think so. She was already on the verge of crying… about losing him.

"I'm tired. It's been a long day, a long week," she said, watching his broad shoulders slump beneath his leather jacket. "I…I'll see you at the office on Monday. Unless you're going back to Topeka."

He shook his head. "I'd rather talk to you outside of the office. If not now, maybe tomorrow."

"What's there to discuss?" She was amazed that she could keep on talking, when everything inside her ached.

"Us."

She met his troubled eyes. "There really isn't an *us*. We both know that." She'd wanted there to be an 'us'.

"So you're moving on already, because I screwed up in the courtroom. Dammit, Antoinette." His expression tightened. "You're going to start seeing Alex, aren't you?"

She'd heard the regret in his voice. But she had to straighten him out about the courtroom matter. "I already told you that I wasn't really mad at you. Mostly I just needed some alone time."

"I still believe that I let you down. I didn't mean to."

"Let it go," she countered.

He gave a curt nod.

"How do you know about Alex asking me out?" Was he jealous? Did she want him to be? Kind of.

He straightened away from her Mustang. "This morning the bastard told me he wanted to ask you out." He swore grimly. "I didn't know he already had."

"Alex isn't a 'bastard'. He's your friend and a nice guy." She gave him a disapproving look. She had her answer to the matter of his being jealous. It made her… What? Happy? Yes. Alex would be a good man to go out with, but he wasn't Chad. He wasn't the man who owned her heart.

Chad moved in front of her, gazed down, and said anxiously, "I don't want you going out with anyone else."

Hope soared through her, but she tried to control it. "Why not?"

He cupped her face with cold hands and kissed her. Kissed her until she was breathless, until she melted against him. *This* was what she'd missed. *This* man, his kisses…everything about him.

Finally he eased back, pulling in steadying breaths. His eyes looked serious, as did his expression. "Because I love you."

The admission wasn't as sweet as she'd hoped it would be. She knew instinctively that he'd felt forced to say it, afraid his best friend would take her out. *Be strong.* "I told Alex no and I won't change my mind. But I can't be with you again, Chad. It's tearing me apart that you're moving away, even if I know it is right for you."

She stepped back, hurting all over. She could be strong for him; for herself.

He moved close again, whispering a finger over her sensitized lips, then smoothing it down her left cheek. "I'm not leaving here."

"Why not?" It didn't make sense. "The opportunity will be good for you. You won't have to keep driving back and forth to Topeka several times a month. That's too dangerous."

"I'm not leaving, and my decision is made. I already told the others no." He gave her a hopeful smile. "Because I have more than enough work here. And because I'm planning on spending a lot less time working. I need better balance in my life."

She felt confused, hopeful. "You've needed to cut back. You've been exhausted so many times. I worry about you."

He studied her intently. "Do you care about me, other than being worried about my lack of sleep?"

Could she admit her true feelings? It frightened her a bit.

"I've already talked to your father," he said, while she remained silent.

She blinked. "My father? What about?"

He went down to one knee in front of her and took her trembling hand in his. "About my intentions toward you. Do you know what he told me?"

She shook her head, speechless with anticipation and love for the man on his knee at her feet.

"He said it was about damn time." A hint of amusement danced in his eyes.

"He didn't say *damn*," she contradicted.

He shrugged. "Okay, I added that part on my own. But I'm sure it was what he'd been thinking."

"I can't believe you talked to my father about us, about whatever your intentions are."

Frustration filled his dear face. "Will you shut up for a moment? Give me a chance to finish what I'm trying to do."

Behind them, Elsie Mae walked out of the café. "I knew it! I knew it, Harold. I told you that he was going to figure things out." When her husband stepped beside her, she ordered, "Get to it already."

Toni started to turn toward her older friend, but Chad stopped her. "Really? You're going to look at someone else when I'm down here on my knee?"

"Spit it out, young man," Harold blustered.

She didn't particularly want an audience, but they were right. She needed him to ask his question before he got annoyed with not being alone and changed his mind.

He chose to ignore them. "I've loved you most of my life, Antoinette. I missed my chance six years ago to ask you out. But I'll be damned if I lose you twice."

Tears slipped down her face and she watched him struggle with his question, *The Question*. She reached down to stroke his beard stubbled face and smiled to prod him along.

The idiot man just knelt there, looking at her.

She took the matter into her own hands and went down to one knee as well. Good thing she'd worn jeans.

His brow furrowed. "What are you doing?"

"Spitting it out, as Harold encouraged. I'm asking you to take a chance on love again." She watched his beautiful blue eyes darken with longing. "I won't let you down. I promise." She leaned toward him, lowering her voice and added in a rush, "And I want a baby as soon as possible."

She held her breath as his eyes widened in surprise and uncertainty. She hadn't meant to say that, but at that moment she'd decided she wanted a baby - his baby - desperately. With her new home, his love, and a child, her life would be complete. She worried her lower lip until suddenly his expression softened.

"So do I," his voice cracked as he spoke. His eyes glistened with emotion.

Elsie Mae and Harold moved beside them. Elsie asked impatiently, "Well, what did he say?" Then she frowned at Chad. "*You* were supposed to do the asking. You were supposed to propose."

He smiled at them and focused on Toni again. "I will, eventually." He stood and pulled her up and into his embrace. He kissed her, with every bit as much passion as he had minutes ago.

"What did he say? Eventually?" Elsie Mae grouched.

Harold huffed. "Give them a chance, woman. If they need to take small steps, we're gonna let them."

She snorted. "Well, are you two together, or not?"

Chad leaned back but continued to hold Toni close. He grinned, nodding. "Definitely *yes*." Then he focused on Toni. "Can you live with 'eventually' for now?"

Toni blinked at her tears, grinned. "I can."

They hadn't noticed that a small crowd had gathered around them. When she heard the footsteps moving closer, she glanced up in surprise. Ted and Alex stood there, grinning and nodding in approval. Ethan, too, smiled at them, looking very pleased. And her parents were there as well. Her Mom was crying and beaming at the same time, just like Elsie Mae was doing.

Her father met Chad's eyes. "When we had a heart-to-heart earlier, he promised that he would never hurt you, daughter. I'll be holding him to that." He motioned to the others. "We'll *all* be watching to make sure he doesn't."

"He won't," Toni said confidently in Chad's defense. "He loves me with his whole stubborn heart. I knew it even when he refused to admit it." But she'd been willing to let him go if that was what he really needed.

He hugged her closer. "Forever and ever, Antoinette. I'll love you the rest of my life and beyond."

Nobody pressed them about an actual proposal, although her father gave Chad a pointed look. She didn't care when it finally happened. He was her man; she was his woman.

Epilogue

Toni put her hands to her lower back and rubbed. She stood in the middle of the front lawn, freshly sodded a couple of months ago and already browning in preparation for the end of another season. New gardens, too, had been planted along the long porch and beside the walkway. So much progress had been made on her new home.

When she'd first stood in this very spot seven months ago, the lawn had been nothing but a few spots of grass and a lot of bare dirt. The house had almost looked worse. But she'd had such visions of what it could become with a lot of TLC. Now the siding had been repaired and painted. The rotten wood of the porch had been fixed and the boards no longer creaked when you walked across them. The chimney on each of the two fireplaces had been rebuilt. And Alex and his crew had added a rounded gazebo on the end of the porch, which had been her favorite part of the Victorian house she'd loved for so many years. Actually, that had been Chad's special gift to her.

There was still a lot to do, since the inside had been as much of a wreck as the outside. But it had reached the point where she and Chad could finally move in. They'd been living together at his small cottage for the last eight months. But this house was where she wanted to live the rest of their lives together and he understood that.

"Don't even think about it," Alex commanded as he walked from around the side of the house with her brother. They both carried massive pumpkins she'd bought recently to sit with a half dozen smaller ones close to the foot of the porch. He'd been watching her like an old mother hen while Chad was away for a month traveling all over the country, promoting some new elder abuse legislation. He was almost worse in his constant attention than Chad.

Alex had caught her looking at the ladder in the front flowerbed; ready to start hanging the string of black and orange lights lying on the ground next to it. She looked at the ladder again, mainly just to tease him. She wouldn't really climb it in her current condition. Being six months pregnant, she tried not to overdo things, although no one seemed to believe her.

"No way are you getting up on that ladder. Chad would skin us alive if we didn't stop you."

"A bit of an exaggeration, don't you think?" she countered, smiling sassily at the man who had come to mean a lot to her. He'd admitted to envying his good buddy for finally stepping up and pushing their relationship forward. But it hadn't hurt his and Chad's friendship. Their bond was stronger than that. She looked at him as a trusted friend, too.

"Maybe, but not by much." He set his heavy burden down where she'd informed him it needed to go. Then he walked closer, his handsome face tight with concern. "Are you feeling okay? I can tell your back is hurting."

The man noticed everything and worried about her more than he should. He'd be a great husband, a wonderful father. If only he could find a woman to meet the ridiculous list of requirements he'd come up with for a suitable wife. Idiot man. She was determined to find someone special for him, in spite of those beyond sensible requirements. She worried about him.

"I'm all right, Mr. Worry Wart. My lower back aches a little, but then I'm walking around carrying all this baby weight." She'd waited until she made it successfully through the first trimester before they'd told their family and friends. Keeping Chad quiet about it had been a struggle. The man was so proud, so happy. She was as well.

Alex grinned and glanced at her rounded stomach. "I can't believe you're having twins. I'm not sure my buddy deserves that much happiness." Except she knew that he was glad his friend was finally moving on from the past.

Her father stepped out of the house onto the porch with her mother. They'd been putting up the Halloween decorations she'd gone a bit crazy purchasing for the surprise welcome home party for Chad the next night. Chad, Ted, and Alex had thoroughly enjoyed Halloween. Especially the 'tricking' part on their friends and neighbors. She'd enjoyed getting a new costume each year and going to parties, or having one at her family's home. She wanted this night to be extra special for Chad and for all of their friends and family.

Her gaze shifted back to the string of lights, ready to be hung along the porch railing.

"Not a chance, daughter. We'll take care of it. You should go inside and lie down a while." Her father was concerned about her and eager to finally be a grandfather.

Her mother looked gently at her. "Or you could decorate the cookies I just baked."

When they'd shown up this morning to help her, they'd brought the Halloween decorations she'd treasured while growing up. And ever since she'd mentioned to Elsie Mae at the café last week that she wanted to decorate the house as a surprise for Chad and have a party, so many people in town had stopped by to drop off a decoration for them. She'd been fully accepted back into the community and had made friends again. And Chad hadn't known it, but a lot of the town had been worried about him.

"I'd rather help out here."

"Stubborn woman," Alex grumbled.

She laughed. "You sound like Chad." She missed him so much she ached inside.

Alex's eyes warmed. "He's a good man." He lowered his voice and asked, "Have you told him yet?"

Actually she'd only told Chad about her decision to set a wedding date. He had asked The Question months ago, but she'd known that he wasn't really ready for that big step. But as her pregnancy advanced, he'd begun letting the pain of his past go. He looked forward to his babies. And he'd started nagging her about getting married before the children were born. She'd made the date decision last night while watching a movie with Alex. Their friend had been relieved and happy for them.

"I'm going to tell him tomorrow night, after the party."

The loud roar of a powerful motorcycle coming in their direction captured her attention, probably everyone else's as well. Beside her Alex stiffened. He inched closer protectively as the bike stopped in front of the house.

It took Toni a couple of seconds before she recognized the visitor as one of her college friends. But as the petite woman climbed off the big Harley and pulled off her helmet, she hesitated in shock. Her friend's beautiful waist-length hair had gone from blonde to bright shades of pink. It made her smile and hurry across the yard.

"Dakota!" The other woman hugged her carefully because of her enormous stomach. "I thought you'd changed your mind about coming."

She would be staying temporarily in Chad's house.

Dakota Endsley shook her head, the thick mass of hair swaying around her slender form. "Just running behind a little."

Alex walked up and studied her friend, his brow pinched, looking disapproving. Dakota frowned right back. Toni had forgotten they'd met years ago when Dakota had come here with her over a short college break. He'd been home on leave at the time and somehow they'd gone out one night. They'd avoided each other after that. When she'd asked her friend about what had happened, Dakota refused to talk about it. So she'd put it out of her thoughts.

"I guess it's time for me to leave. Duties I should get to." Alex shot a final scowl at Dakota and hurried to his truck parked down the street. He hadn't even bothered to tell the others goodbye. And Toni knew he had taken the day off.

"Hmmm, that will be interesting," she said quietly, gazing at Dakota.

"What?" Dakota asked, continuing to watch Alex walk away. There was something wounded in her gaze, making Toni even more curious.

"You two being in the wedding party. You'll be my maid of honor. He'll be Chad's best man."

Dakota started to respond, but instead smiled hugely, looking at something behind Toni.

Toni's heart raced as she recognized who had walked up behind her. She knew his smell, his walk. Somehow Chad had arrived and intended to surprise her. She flung herself at him. "Why didn't you tell me you were coming early?" But she didn't really care. She was just so happy he was home.

He grinned. "Wanted to surprise my woman." He looked curious from her to Dakota and back. "Did I hear you two talking about a wedding party? Whose party?"

She'd wanted to tell him her decision in private, but just like the proposal incident, they were going to have an audience. Ethan and her parents moved closer. Ted and Elsie Mae, who had been helping inside the house, stopped next to them. Everyone looked at her expectantly.

She sighed, looking up at Chad in resignation. "*Our* wedding party. But it's not actually a party. I'm talking about who will stand up with us when we get married."

"Married?" he asked in surprise, beaming. "You're finally going to make an honest man of me."

She nodded, barely able to control her excitement. "I've decided we're both ready now." She giggled and patted her stomach. "Well, *all* of us are ready."

He swept her off her feet and swung her around, then set her down, gasping, "Damn. I shouldn't have done that. Are you all right? Are the babies okay?"

"We're fine." She motioned toward the house, ready to share her other surprise with him. "We've been decorating for Halloween. We're having a party here tomorrow night." She lightly punched his arm. "It was supposed to be a surprise for you."

He studied the partially decorated house, the gathering of family and friends, and looked back at her. Tears glistened in his eyes. "Thank you."

"I love you, you know. With all my heart," she said as her voice shook.

"As do I, sweetheart. More with every passing day." Then he grinned again. "A Halloween party. Really? It's been a long time since..."

He thumped his forehead, looking sheepish. "I got distracted, sorry. So when is my big day? The one I've been waiting patiently for."

"Impatiently waiting for," she countered, with a chuckle. "*Our* big day will be on Thanksgiving Day. I want to celebrate that day with our friends and family. I want everyone to know how very thankful I am for coming home and finding the man of my heart."

Everyone moved around them, talking all at once, excited that they were finally setting a date. Even Alex returned to share in the moment, but he kept his distance from Dakota. She would have to find out about what had happened between them. Whatever it was, they both were wary now of each other.

Chad scooped her up into his arms. He looked at the others with clear intent. "How about we finish this decorating stuff tomorrow? I want some private time with the woman who has at long last agreed to drag me to church for a wedding."

The crowd laughed and Toni bopped him lightly in the shoulder. "You're going to pay for that."

He focused on her as the others moved away. "I hope so, Antoinette. I hope you wear me out trying to make me pay for the taunt."

"Oh, I will. Count on it."

The end

About the author

Starla wears many hats professionally and as a writer. She is the community coordinator for a Midwestern accounting firm, a gerontologist who volunteers with an active group of senior adults, a mentor/teacher of writing and a multi-published author. She dabbles in writing romances of many sub-genres: contemporary, historical Western, medieval, sci-fi, fantasy, paranormal and Regency. To date she has published 20 novels, 37 novellas, 7 anthologies and 15 short stories.

Also by Starla Kaye

Their Lady Gloriana
Holly's Big Bad Santa
Cowboys in Charge
Her Cowboy's Way

www.ingramcontent.com/pod-product-compliance
Lightning Source LLC
Chambersburg PA
CBHW030336020726
47493CB00004B/1291